www.terrypratchett.co.uk

GREENWICH LIBRARIES

3 8028 02411978 3

the fantastically funny

TERRY PRATCHETT

The
WITCH'S
Vacuum Cleaner
and other stories

CORGI BOOKS

CORGI BOOKS

UK | USA | Canada | Ireland | Australia
India | New Zealand | South Africa

Corgi Books is part of the Penguin Random House group of companies
whose addresses can be found at global.penguinrandomhouse.com.

www.penguin.co.uk   www.puffin.co.uk   www.ladybird.co.uk

First published by Doubleday 2016
Published by Corgi Books 2017

005

Text copyright © Terry and Lyn Pratchett, 2016
Illustrations by Mark Beech; copyright © The Random House Group Ltd, 2016

All stories contained in this collection were originally published in the 'Children's Circle'
section of the *Bucks Free Press* in the following publication years. All stories were previously
untitled, and so these titles have been attributed for the purposes of this collection.

'The Witch's Vacuum Cleaner' (1970); 'The Great Train Robbery' (1966); 'The Truly Terrible
Toothache' (1973); 'The Frozen Feud' (1967); 'Darby and the Submarine' (1966); 'The
Sheep Rodeo Scandal' (1969); 'An Ant called 4179003' (1970); 'The Fire Opal' (1968);
'Lord Cake and the Battle for Banwen's Beacon' (1968); 'The Time-travelling Television'
(1972); 'The Blackbury Park Statues' (1970); 'Wizard War' (1968); 'The Extraordinary
Adventures of Doggins' (1966); 'Rincemangle, the Gnome of Even Moor' (1973)

Discworld® is a trademark registered by Terry Pratchett

Set in Minister Light
Printed and bound in Great Britain by Clays Ltd, Elcograf S.p.A.

A CIP catalogue record for this book is available from the British Library

ISBN: 978-0-552-57449-5

All correspondence to:
Corgi Books, Penguin Random House Children's
80 Strand, London WC2R 0RL

And so the journey begins, young Terry.
Who knows where it will take you?
Enjoy the ride!

Terry Pratchett
Salisbury, UK

CONTENTS

INTRODUCTION

Do you believe in magic? Can you imagine a war between wizards? An exciting journey in an airship, or down in a submarine? Would you like to meet the fastest truncheon in the Wild West?

If *yes*, then these stories are for you. There are all of the above, as well as a witch flying about on a vacuum cleaner, some walking talking statues, a rebel ant – and a massive pie! One of these stories was even the birth of the idea which led later to my longer book, *Truckers*.

The stories were written way back when I was a lad working as a junior reporter, and they were published weekly in my local newspaper. The young readers then weren't like you in lots of ways – they had no computer tablets or games consoles and fish and chips was the only takeaway in town. But they were *exactly* the same in that they wanted to read about other worlds, about strange creatures and characters, about extraordinary journeys and magic battles.

I've tinkered here and there with a few details, added a few lines or notes, just because I can – and because as I've got older my imagination has got even bigger so I can't stop myself adding bits and bobs. But the stories in this collection are all mostly as they were first printed.

And enjoyed.

By anyone with an imagination . . .

Terry Pratchett,
Wiltshire 2015

THE WITCH'S VACUUM CLEANER

Mr Ronald 'Uncle Ron' Swimble liked birthdays because they meant parties, and since he was a part-time conjuror that meant engagements. He could make eggs appear out of nowhere, pull flags of all nations out of people's ears, do fifty different card tricks and was generally very good at the sort of magic that's

learned by hard practice in front of a mirror.*
He was President of the Blackbury Magic
Rectangle too.

Uncle Ron had a
parrot called Mimms
who could pick cards
out of a hat and liked to
shout, and a daughter called

Lucy who generally stood on the stage saying very
little, but who took his cloak and handed him
Mimms in a cage and so on.

All three were very happy until the night of
Jimmy Waddle's tenth birthday party at the town
hall.

Uncle Ron walked onto the stage, and all the
children bellowed,

'Hello, Uncle Ron!'

* And even harder practice in front of people, for not many mirrors shout
things like 'Rubbish!' And if your mirror does, you probably don't need to
worry about whether or not you can learn to do magic tricks. Knowing how
to run away very fast would be a more useful skill.

and then his hat fell off and three rabbits tumbled out.

He bent down to pick them up and a flock of pigeons burst out of his jacket, a daffodil shot out of his ear and his bow tie began to revolve at high speed. It was all very entertaining, and young Jimmy Waddle was wide-eyed with amazement, but the most surprised person in the hall was Uncle Ron. They weren't his tricks, and anyway, he was allergic to rabbits.

He tried to carry on, but his act went all to pot. He did plenty of tricks, like turning a top hat into a vase of flowers and making a table disappear. But he didn't mean

3

to. Every time he moved his hands something appeared or vanished. He was almost in tears by the time he reached for his pack of cards, and when that turned into a glass of wine he ran off the stage.

'That's a new lot—' began Lucy.

'They're not mine! I don't know what's happening! I haven't even got any pigeons!'

'Cake!' screamed Mimms.

The audience was still clapping, and Ronald had to go and take two bows before he could say any more. Everyone was shaking his hand and asking him how he did it.

Finally he reached his dressing room and locked the door.

'I don't know how it happened,' he said. 'But it was as if all I had to do was point my finger at something, like that cupboard there, and say "Turn into a hat stand" and—'

It turned into a hat stand.

'Jam!' screamed Mimms.

Ronald pointed his finger at his hat.

'Vanish,' he said hoarsely. It did.

*

They went home by taxi. Every now and again Ron would point his finger at things on the pavement, just to see if the magic was still there – and three lampposts were turned into a stork, a small yellow elephant on wheels, and a baby's buggy.

The trouble came when he paid the taxi driver. Because although Uncle Ron could turn things into other things, he didn't have much control over what might change, *or* what something would turn into. So when he took his wallet out of his pocket it suddenly became a cheese sandwich. Lucy had to pay the fare out of her lunch money and the taxi driver drove off hurriedly.

'The front-door key is in my waistcoat pocket,' said Ron through clenched teeth. 'I don't think I can touch things any more. You'd better unlock the door in case I turn it into something unmentionable.'

'Gloves!' said Lucy. 'That's it! Put a pair on, and then you'll be able to touch things again.'

'I haven't got any,' Ron said miserably. 'And if I had they'd turn into something as soon as I touched them.'

Lucy fetched a pair of her red woolly ones, with daft rabbits embroidered in odd colours on the back. Sure enough, as soon as Ron touched them they changed – into socks. That gave her an idea. She went and got a pair of her father's socks, and sure enough again, these changed into red woolly gloves as soon as he put them on his hands.

Ron slumped down onto a chair and picked up the phone. He asked some of his fellow conjurors from Blackbury Magic Rectangle to come round at once, and soon the little house was filled with people.

'Watch this,' Ron told them, taking his gloves off

and pointing at a little potted cactus. It turned into a bowl of marbles! Everyone gasped satisfactorily except for one woman, who had just looked out of the window and seen a small wheeled elephant trundling by towing a stork on a baby's buggy.

'It's not trickery,' said Ron. 'It's the real thing – proper magic.'

'Marmalade!' Mimms screeched.

'There's no such thing,' scoffed Amir Raj, who did card tricks.

'It's all illusion,' added Presto Changeo, who sawed his assistant in half twice nightly.

'Sandwich!' screamed Mimms, rapping his beak against his cage.

Ronald turned the table into a lawn mower.

'What can I do?' he said. 'I could make my fortune, I suppose, but I don't want to have to wear gloves all the time. And anyway, I might turn

something good into something dreadful.'

'Could it have been anything you've eaten? Did anything unusual happen today?' asked Presto.

'Let's see now . . . not much. The only thing unusual that I can remember is knocking over an old lady's vacuum cleaner when I went to work this morning. It was in the car park – no idea why. She went on something dreadful about it, but she *had* leaned it against my car.'

'Was it a small lady with a brown coat and a sort of flowerpot hat full of hat pins?' asked Lucy, who had been listening to all this. 'It was? Oh dear, oh dear – I never thought of that. That's Mrs Riley, and she's a witch.'*

'Biscuits! Crisps! Ice cream!'

came from Mimms.

'You mean she's put a spell on me?' said Ron, ignoring his parrot.

---

* Something that every child in the town knew for a fact, though strangely not known by a single grown-up.

'That's ridiculous, magic doesn't exist—' began Presto Changeo, and stopped when Ron turned a pencil into a small banana.

'I think that just proved otherwise,' said Ron, picking up the banana and absentmindedly peeling it. 'The question is, what can we do about it?'

'Go round and plead with her,' said Presto practically.

So Uncle Ron and the other Blackbury conjurors set out for Mrs Riley's house, which was No. 3 Dahlia Crescent, and didn't look much as though it belonged to a witch – there were lots of pretty flowers in the front garden, for instance.

Lucy rang the bell twice, and Presto hammered on the door. They peered through the windows, but couldn't see very much as she seemed to have a small forest of houseplants on the sill inside.

'It's no good, she must be asleep or out,' said Ron.

There was a noise above them like a vacuum cleaner. It *was* a vacuum cleaner, and it was hovering in the air with Mrs Riley straddling it. A jet of dust was shooting out, keeping it aloft.

'Oh, it's you, Swimble,' she said. 'I suppose you've come round to beg me to take the spell off?'

'If you don't mind—' began Ron, staring at the vacuum cleaner.

'I certainly do! Anyway, you're a conjuror, always making out that you can do magic – so get rid of the spell yourself!'

'We don't do that kind of magic, ma'am,' said Presto.

She peered angrily at him. **'You don't even believe in it!'** she snapped. **'Cats' teeth! Card tricks and rabbits out of hats? You're a lot of arrogant usurpers!'**

'Eh?'

'She means you're intruding where you're not wanted,' said Lucy. 'Come away, Dad, before she gets too angry.'

The vacuum cleaner roared and started to rise again.

'What a remarkable lady,' said Ron admiringly, watching the witch zoom away over the rooftops. 'Is there a Mr Riley? Oh, he got lost at sea, eh? Well, well, she sure is a fine woman.'

That night Ron found it was very uncomfortable to sleep wearing woolly gloves, but he couldn't take them off in case he turned the bed into a knife rack or a horse.

What on earth am I going to do? he wondered. Ron had to take the next day off his ordinary job because of his magic hands. Lucy phoned up the factory where her father worked, and said he had flu, because she thought it was better to tell his boss that than the unbelievable truth.

Presto Changeo came round at lunch time. 'I've got an idea,' he said. 'Can't we get the vicar to do something?'

'Mrs Riley is in the choir, and she's embroidered thousands of kneelers,' sighed Lucy. 'Reverend Cowparslie would never believe she's a witch. Anyway, she's a nice old soul at heart, just a bit bad-tempered. I quite like her, actually.'

'Perhaps if I went round to see her with a box of chocs and some flowers she might forgive me,' said Ron, blushing.

'Bananas!' screamed Mimms.

'And to think I see her every week when she comes in to change her library books,' said Presto, who worked in the library. 'They're not even magic books, either. Just novels about doctors – *you* know the sort, *Doctor Fingdangle and the Angel of Ward Ten* or *Love Among the Bedpans* – and books on gardening, like *My Troublesome Fig and Other Terrible Torments*. If I hadn't seen her on her vacuum cleaner, I'd never have believed she was a witch.'

'Pizza!' added Mimms.*

'Gardening, eh?' murmured Ron, who knew his nettles from his nightshade.† 'I have an idea . . .'

After lunch he put on his best clothes, polished his top hat, stuck a few tricks in his pockets and set out for Mrs Riley's neat little house.

She opened the door a fraction after he'd knocked umpteen times.

'Oh, it's you,' she said. 'Go away before I—'

'Mrs Riley, I want to see you,' he said. 'Please let me come in or I shall take my gloves off and turn

* Sadly for Mimms, Ron's skills did not seem to include turning a bowl of sunflower seeds into pizza. Or even bananas.
† And even his Nanki-Poo Azalea from his Nature's Mistake.

your door knocker into a penguin!'

'Wipe your feet, then.'

Sitting among the tiny tables and highly polished furniture in her little front room, peering at the witch through her little jungle of pot plants, Ron said: 'Mrs Riley, you see before you a bewildered man. Everything I touch won't stay the same. It's getting on my nerves, and I'm very sorry, and, erm . . . erm . . . Mrs Riley, will you marry me?'

'**Good heavens!**' said Mrs Riley, as Ron produced a small Purple Passion houseplant out of mid-air.

'Ever since my dear wife died I've been looking for another lady who really understood magic,' said Ron, producing a box of chocolates from his top hat. 'Marry me, Mrs Riley, and I'll be the happiest conjuror in Blackbury – and if you could see your way clear to taking your spell off me I'd be glad.'

Mrs Riley blew her nose. 'Well, this *is* sudden,' she said.

'Say yes, Mrs Riley, or I will throw myself into the Blackbury Municipal Boating Lake!' cried Ron.

'Yes,' she said.

The wedding was a quiet one, and Presto Changeo, who was Best Man, lost the ring but produced a string of flags of all nations, a box of eggs, pigeons, a pack of cards, glasses and ping-pong balls from his pockets instead.

Then the happy couple walked out of the church under an archway of top hats and broomsticks. The Rev. Arnold Cowparslie, the vicar, thought that was a bit unusual but said nothing – even when Ron and his new wife rode off on a vacuum cleaner decorated with tin cans and ribbons.

Led by Lucy, everyone cheered.

Except for Mimms.

'Brussels sprouts!' he screeched

loudly.*

* And, sadly, Amir Raj waved his hands and produced a bagful as a special
present. If only Mimms had asked for *cake* . . .

THE GREAT
TRAIN ROBBERY

I dare say you all know about the Wild West. But
what many people don't know is that there were two
Wild Wests, and the wilder one by far was in Britain.
Of course, this rough, tough, rip-roaring, gun-sling-
ing place I'm referring to is Wales, and to prove it,
here is the story of Police Constable Bryn Bunyan,
the fastest truncheon west of the River Severn.

The town of Llandanffwnfafegettupagogo was very small, and hardly on the map at all,* until the Great Coal Rush of '81. No sooner had an old prospector come running down the High Street with a lump of coal in his hands, shouting,

'Coal! It's coal! There's coal in them there hills, look you!' than the town was packed with people eager to strike their claim.

Soon it had three pubs, a billiard hall and a brand-new Temperance Hotel.

And every night there were fights between the sheepboys (like cowboys, only this is Wales) and the prospectors. Soon the place became known as 'the toughest town in the West'.

And so it remained, for nigh on a hundred years.

Then one day, with the sunlight glinting on the silver star on his helmet, a tall figure in blue

* Anyone looking for it on a map needed very good eyesight, as to fit the name on meant it had to be printed in very tiny letters.

pedalled down the High Street of Llandanff.

The people in the public bar of the Lump o' Coke peered round the door as the stranger dismounted and tied his bike up outside the old police station.

'It's a policeman!'

hissed Davies the Poacher, gulping down his beer and hurrying off to hide his ferrets.*

* Putting them down his trousers didn't seem like a very good idea.

The news spread like wildfire. Soon it reached the ears of Big Dai Evans,* sheep-stealer, poacher and thief, who was playing billiards. He was the biggest bandit in Llandanff (which is saying a lot) and people wondered how he would take the news.

It also came to the notice of Gorsebush Jones, a young sheep farmer and poacher.

Later that day there was a knock on the police-station door.

'What can I do for you?' asked PC Bunyan, as a rather scrawny lad entered.

'Look you,' said Gorsebush hurriedly. 'Big Dai Evans is after you . . .' He looked quite frightened, and the wispy hairs on his chin were quivering.

Now Gorsebush knew there was a reason why Dai Evans didn't want any police around. He was planning to rob the noon train to Cardiff as it went through Llandanff Halt!

* Son of the famed outlaw Dai Orribly, who had lived up to his name, and brother to Dai Too, who was trying *not* to live up to his.

Poor old Gorsebush knew about this, and his old granny was on that train and he didn't want to see her get hurt. Pausing every few moments to peer over his shoulder, he told the policeman all about it.

PC Bunyan listened hard, and made some calls. Then he decided to go and see for himself. Ask a few questions.

And there was more trouble to come. Because when PC Bunyan made his rounds a few minutes later, with Gorsebush following him, he happened to go past the Lump o' Coke.

There was a bike outside. Swiftly testing it, the policeman found that neither the brakes nor the lights were working. He went in to find the owner, while Gorsebush sat trembling outside, then turned tail and scuttled off. You see, he knew that bike belonged to Big Dai.

There was dead silence as PC Bunyan pushed open the door.

There, leaning on the bar, was Big Dai, enjoying a glass of leek beer and a packet of crisps. People began to edge away and one or two scrambled through the door, suddenly remembering important business elsewhere. Jones the bottle-collector ducked down behind the till. Someone stopped playing the piano.

'Is that your bike outside, sir?' asked PC Bunyan. You could have heard a pin drop.

'Yes,' said Big Dai.

'I must warn you, sir, that the brakes don't work, and it has no lights. You cannot ride it after dark unless you get it repaired.'

Everyone looked at Big Dai. No one had ever talked to him like that before, ever told him what to do.

'Thank you, Officer,' he said at last. 'Then I won't ride it home tonight.'

Well! They were expecting a punch-up at least!

Dai called his rascally bandits together after the policeman had left. 'Don't you see, look you,' he hissed. 'We don't want any trouble with the police, not with the train robbery and all.'

Then the gang crept out through the back door, to where the rails of the railway track gleamed under the rising moon.

PC Bunyan went back to the warm police station. There was a large sheepdog in front of the stove, and from the sound of it, there were sheep in the cells.

Gorsebush Jones had been

making himself at home.*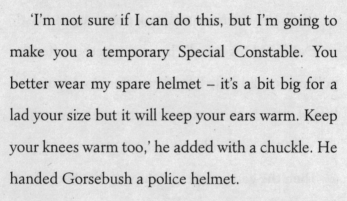

'Gorsebush!'

'Yessir!' said Gorsebush.

'I'm not sure if I can do this, but I'm going to make you a temporary Special Constable. You better wear my spare helmet – it's a bit big for a lad your size but it will keep your ears warm. Keep your knees warm too,' he added with a chuckle. He handed Gorsebush a police helmet.

'What about Blodwen?' came the muffled voice from under the helmet. 'She'd make a good police dog, wouldn't she?'

'Very well. But she'll have to do without a helmet. Now come on, we must get to the railway station. I aim to tidy up this town.'

* Hiding, actually.

And so two men and a dog left Llandanff-wnfafegettupagogo on one bicycle. In the distance, PC Bunyan heard a train whistle, and knew that it was the Cardiff train. What devilish scheme did Dai Evans have in mind for stopping it?

Gorsebush jumped off the bike and examined the ground. 'Some bikes went by here not two hours ago, boyo,' he said.*

'Riding without lights, eh?' muttered PC Bunyan. 'And I warned the scoundrel of that!'

Swiftly they pedalled onwards. The Cardiff train

---

* If you think tracking cowboys by the tracks of their horses is hard, well, you should try following bikes over the Welsh mountains by the light of the moon.

would have to slow down as it passed Llandanff, and that's where Big Dai would ambush it.

'**Look you, down in the valley,**' shouted Gorsebush above the rushing wind. '**We're too late, boyo!**'

There, shining in the moonlight, was a great heap of coal, right across the railway track. Big Dai was going to derail the Cardiff Express!

Up on the hill PC Bunyan thumbed his three-speed gears into top gear and pedalled like mad! With a *twang!* both brake cables snapped . . .

In the warm cabin of the engine, Driver Tommo Lloyd-George and Fireman Davies were enjoying a nice hot cup of cocoa, freshly brewed on the firebox.

'Now there's something you don't often see,' said Fireman Davies, looking out of the cab windows.

Down the hill, waving and screaming, came a policeman, a young lad in a large helmet, and a barking sheepdog, all on one bicycle. With both axles glowing red hot in the darkness, the bike drew level with the cabin.

'What are they saying?' said the driver.

'It sounded like "Stop the train!", Tommo,' said the fireman.

Gorsebush and PC Bunyan were shouting themselves hoarse, and the bike was gradually losing speed. The train began to slip past them.

'Gorsebush,' shouted PC Bunyan. 'Would you care to jump onto one of the carriages and pull the communication cord?'

'I can't afford the five-pound fine,' moaned Gorsebush.

'I'm sure they'll overlook it. Hurry up!'

Closing his eyes tightly and standing up on the

swaying saddle, Gorsebush took a deep breath and launched himself into space. **Clunk!** He hit the side of the last carriage, and clung to a door handle.

'Excuse me, lady, but I ain't got time for no manners,' he said as he reached in through a first-class compartment window, grabbed the cord and tugged it downwards.

Screech!

The train braked suddenly, and slid to a halt just a few metres from the ambush.

A few seconds later PC Bunyan and Blodwen whizzed up on the bike, crashing right into the bushes where Dai Evans and his gang were hiding.

Gorsebush leaped off the side of the train and ran over too. He began tackling everyone as a shrill police whistle split the air. Over the hill galloped

a squad of mounted policemen, summoned earlier by PC Bunyan.

It was all up now for Big Dai Evans. Blodwen the sheepdog herded the bandits together and they were marched off for a long spell in jail.

And that's about the end of it. PC Bunyan was promoted to Police Sergeant Bunyan for his part in foiling the train robbers. And his assistant in the village was – you've guessed it – PC Gorsebush Jones, who got into the Force by standing on tiptoe and lying about his age. He still went poaching, only now, whenever he caught himself, he arrested himself, charged himself, and let himself go after a stern warning.

Blodwen became Police Dog Blodwen, and soon had the most law-abiding flock in South Wales.

Oh, and Gorsebush's granny arrived safe and well. Only to tell Gorsebush off about the language she had heard him using. *And* to make him shave off the wisps of 'beard' on his chin.

And that was how the town of Llandanff-wnfafegettupagogo was cleaned up, due to the fastest truncheon in the West – PC Bryn Bunyan . . . and Gorsebush Jones, of course.

THE TRULY TERRIBLE TOOTHACHE

It happened on a sunny afternoon in Blackbury. Mr Arnold Suttle, the borough librarian, was sorting out the old books stored in the attic. There were all sorts – a lot of them came to the library from old houses, or jumble sales, and most of them found their way onto the shelves. But there were always one or two which, for one reason or another, were stored in the attic.

'*Every Criminal's Guide to Picking Pockets,*' said Mr Suttle to himself. 'Hm, that'll never do. What's this? *Poaching and Sheep-Stealing for Beginners.* Quite unsuitable. Hello, it's the first time I've seen *this* one.'

He lifted a very dusty volume out of a box. It was bound in leather, with big brass hinges. He wiped the dust off the title which said, in faded gold letters,

THEE MAGICKAL BOKE
OF BLACK WYLLYAM
DE BLACKBYRY.

'How interesting,' said Mr Suttle. He opened it, and on the title page was written in faded brown writing:

Yf ths Boke should dare to roam,
bocks yts ears & sende yt home.

He turned over some more heavy pages, which were covered with writing and pictures of an extremely magical nature.

'I wonder what this means,' he said out loud. 'It looks very magical: "Igni passage inferni ehthonical gil per—"'

A cloud passed over the sun, and there was a roll of thunder. There was also a puff of smoke and a flash of light, which lost its effect because the electric light was on anyway, and a tall black shape appeared from nowhere.

'Blimey!' said Mr Suttle. 'Who are you?'

The man standing before him appeared to be almost completely black because he was wearing a long black coat, a flat black hat, and sported a long black beard.

The man – who looked rather puzzled – said something that Mr Suttle didn't understand. But then he saw the book and his face lit up. He grabbed it and pointed to the name on the cover.

'Black William de Blackbyry?' said Mr Suttle. 'With a magic book? I say,' he said, stepping back a bit, 'are you some sort of wizard or something? Not that I believe in them, of course.'

The man didn't answer, but with a wave of his hand he produced an egg, a three-legged stool and a bundle of silk handkerchiefs.

'That's magic,' said Mr Suttle, who knew it when he saw it, all right.

Black William looked interestedly around the attic, and then looked closely at Mr Suttle. He obviously didn't like what he saw, because he raised one bony arm, said a few words, and something went

bang!

There was a cloud of green smoke and Black William disappeared.

Mr Suttle looked down. He had been wearing an ordinary grey suit. Now he was wearing bright red stockings, baggy pantaloon trousers, a bright green jacket with lots of gold decorations, a belt with a sword on it and – he reached up to his head – a black velvet cap with a feather in it.

'I feel a right silly,' he said,* and sat down.

A few minutes later he crept down from the attic

* He *looked* a right silly too.

to the main library, hoping to slip into his office before anyone noticed him.

But he needn't have worried. Miss Blenkinsop, who usually stamped the books behind the counter, was far too preoccupied. She was wearing a long Elizabethan dress and a wide ruff studded with pearls and amethysts, and a little cap covered with diamonds.

'Don't tell me,' said Mr Suttle. 'A tall man in a black cloak has just been through.'

'That's right, he— Gosh, Mr Suttle, you do look strange in those clothes! Just like Sir Walter Raleigh! What's that book you're holding?'

'I think I may have done something a bit stupid,' the librarian said. 'First of all, I'm going home to change, and then I think I'd better find out something about Black William de Blackbyry.'

He walked to the door of the library and gasped. The street was full of stopped cars. There wasn't a single engine running. And their drivers

stood around in Elizabethan costume, which can be very hampering when you're trying to repair a car.* Some of the houses on the street had changed too, from respectable red brick to half-timbered Tudor.

'By my halberd!' he swore. 'Good heavens! What did I say *that* for?'

Pretty soon Blackbury began to look very odd. Within the first few hours things started to disappear.

* It would also be fair to say that many of the local men did not look very comfortable wearing tights and bloomers in the High Street.

TVs were the first to go, then electricity wires and traffic lights. They just vanished in little flashes of green light.

Meanwhile Mr Suttle and Miss Blenkinsop hurried across to the town hall. The Mayor was there, but instead of his usual dark grey suit he was wearing a very heavy costume which was all gold, purple and furs. Chief Inspector Jethwa was there too. He was dressed as a Tower of London Beefeater and looked rather good as one too.

'No funny remarks,' he said. 'My uniform just turned into this. I keep breaking light bulbs with this spear thing,' he said, flourishing the iron-tipped pike which the ceremonial Beefeaters still carried at the Tower of London. 'Still, there's no electricity so it doesn't really matter.'

'Everything's going old-fashioned,' said the Mayor. 'Up at the army camp – well, they're very bothered. The tanks have turned into brass cannons and the soldiers are having to wear armour and leather breeches. And that isn't the worst.'

Mr Suttle bit his lip. 'Let me guess,' he said. 'I bet that when you try to get out of Blackbury, you can't!'

'Zounds! That's right!' said the Mayor. 'My Lord Chief Inspector Jethwa here was only just saying that a heavy mist hath settled around the town, and all who try enter it find themselves walking back to Blackbyry, by my troth!'

'And thou art talking Elizabethan,' said Mr Suttle, and he sat down suddenly. 'And so am I.' He pushed a pile of books onto the table. 'I hath a sort of idea,' he said. 'Hast thou heard of Black William de Blackbyry?'

They shook their heads.

'I've just been reading about him. He was a famous enchanter who dwelt here in Queen Elizabeth the First's time. I found his book of spells in the library, and when I read it he appeared.

'He's still somewhere in Blackbyry – I meaneth

Blackbury – I mean "mean" – oh dear, I'm finding it hard to concentrate. I think he's trying to turn the town back to how he remembers it. The only things that will, by my troth, be left will be the sort of things that were here four hundred and fifty years ago, or as near as he can get to them.'

'That's a likely story!' said the Mayor. 'Still, I canst not think of a better one.'

'That's another thing,' said Mr Suttle. 'I've got a horrible feeling that if we don't concentrate on remembering what's happened, we really will think we're Elizabethans. That goeth for talking like them too. Black William is trying to get us to do that, methinks.'

Just then there was a horrible **CRASH** above them.

They raced upstairs and found a man sitting on a pile of rubbish in the town-hall attic.

Half a helicopter was sticking through the roof.

The man looked up at them. **'What are you lot dressed up like that for?'** he cried in astonishment.

'You don't look all that ordinary yourself,' said Mr Suttle, since the man was wearing leather armour. He climbed up a rafter to look more closely at the helicopter.

'I was wearing a respectable RAF uniform five minutes ago!' said the pilot. 'What's going on? I was sent to fly over to see why people couldn't get into Blackbury. There's a mist all around the town.'

They told him, but he didn't believe them.

'It's true,' said Mr Suttle. 'I bet your helicopter just stopped suddenly, did it not? Nothing seemed to work.'

'By God, you speaketh true! Not even the radio!'

'I think I'm beginning to understand Black William,' said Mr Suttle, rubbing his hands together. 'You see, helicopters and radios and such would sound absolutely impossible to a man from four hundred and fifty years ago, so as far as he is concerned they don't exist. They just stop working.'

'I've been thinking about it, and I'm not sure I wouldn't mind living in Elizabethan times. They were pretty exciting,' said the Mayor. He looked down at his outfit. 'And I do rather *like* this costume.'

'But we're not back in Elizabethan times really,' said Mr Suttle. 'We're – well, inside a magic spell.'

'Let's find this Black William and make him see

reason,' said Chief Inspector Jethwa, and Mr Suttle hurried off with him while the other two helped the pilot.

Blackbury had changed even more, but most of the people in the streets didn't seem to realize it. A fair had appeared, with jugglers and dancing bears, and some men were holding an archery competition outside what had been the Blackbury Co-op.

'It's rather jolly,' said Chief Inspector Jethwa grudgingly.

'I dunno,' murmured Mr Suttle. 'No proper doctors, no clean drinking water . . . pretty chancy, if you ask me.'

They hired a pair of horses at a stable which had appeared on the site of the Blackbury Whizzo Garage.

'According to the Blackbury history books, Black William used to live in a castle on Even Moor,' said Mr Suttle. 'But we'd better watch our step! He probably believed in all sorts of things – witches and giants, and demons. We'd better be prepared for them to be about.'

'But they never really existed,' protested Chief Inspector Jethwa.

'I know, but if he thought they did, they do now – so watch out!'

They rode towards Even Moor in search of Black William. It was a rather odd ride. The country had suddenly become very wild, but here and there were bits of the twenty-first century that Black William had left untouched by mistake – a letter box, several hundred metres of railway track, and a piece of road, complete with white lines, on a bumpy cart track.

Mr Suttle was reading Black William's big magical book as he rode, while Chief Inspector Jethwa glanced nervously around.

'As far as I can make out, Black William magicked himself into nothingness until someone came along to read the spell,' the librarian said.

'By my troth, I wishe I was out of thys playce—' began Chief Inspector Jethwa.

'Careful! You're speaking Elizabethan!' said Mr Suttle. 'Concentrate! You don't want to fall under the spell, or we'll never get out!'

At that moment a fire-breathing demon, four metres high, jumped out of the bushes and roared at them.

Chief Inspector Jethwa fell off his horse. 'But I don't believe in them! They don't exist!' he cried.

'Black William thinks they do, and that's all that matters,' said Mr Suttle. He had a quick think, and then pointed a finger at the demon, which seemed to be trying to spread Chief Inspector Jethwa with mustard. There was a fizz, and fierce blue flames surrounded the demon like a cage. It ran away, screaming.

'I used magic!' said Mr Suttle, helping the other man back onto his horse. 'Black William thinks it exists, so it does. And I can do it too.'

Ten minutes later they found the wizard's house. It was a big Tudor mansion on the edge of a wood, and it appeared to be glowing. There seemed to be a lot more magic in the air. Mr Suttle had to concentrate very hard to stop thinking in Elizabethan.

'I hope you're ready,' he said.

'Aye,' said Chief Inspector Jethwa. 'I mean, yes.'

Mr Suttle **knocked** on the big oak door.

It swung open. Mr Suttle and Chief Inspector Jethwa crept in rather nervously, but the big hall inside was quite ordinary. It was lined with oak panels and there were several suits of armour standing about.

'Now to find Black William,' said Mr Suttle. They decided to climb the ornate staircase. It was a little difficult, because Inspector Jethwa was trying to keep as close as possible to Mr Suttle. Shadows loomed in the dark corners.

'Half a mo',' said Mr Suttle, opening the magic book. 'There's a spell in here about light. Ah yes, um:

"MARAZDA IGNIFEROUS! WHIZA TUNGSTUNFILMANTLE"!'

A bright green glow appeared in the air, and followed them up the stairs. At the top they found another door, and pushed it open. A pungent pong came from within.

They had discovered Black William's magic workshop. It was a high-ceilinged room, lit by a fire in a brass cauldron. Magic swords filled an umbrella stand. There were cupboards and cupboards crammed with jars of strange and wonderful ingredients – unicorn horns, dried beetles, shavings of camels' toenails and cabbages.* Magic circles and signs of the zodiac were painted on the walls, along with chalked cabbage recipes that the wizard must have done in a moment of absent-mindedness. There was a bookcase crammed with old leather books, and Mr Suttle whistled when he saw the titles.

*These are surprisingly magical, so must be handled very carefully.

'This lot would be worth a fortune,' he said.

Apart from all that, the room was empty. The only sound was from the fire, when the coals settled.

'Supposing the wizard comes back?' said Chief Inspector Jethwa.

'Well, he didn't look a bad sort,' said Mr Suttle. 'I wouldn't mind meeting him.'

Suddenly there was a *whoomph!* and the wizard appeared in a cloud of yellow smoke, which rather lost its effect in Mr Suttle's magical green light. Black William didn't look very fearsome either. In fact, he looked very fed up. He was clutching the side of his face and moaning.

'I say, what's up, old chap?' said Mr Suttle.

The wizard just moaned. 'For four hundred and fifty years, this tooth here hast given me more grief than a herd of rampaging boars!'

'Good heavens! I believe he's got toothache,' said Mr Suttle.

'By my tooth! I mean, by my troth!' Black William exclaimed.

'Poor old chap. Have you tried anything for it?'

'All sorts of things,' muttered Black William. 'Toothwart, boiled beans in wine, and incantations by the light of the moon.'

Chief Inspector Jethwa relaxed. A wizard with a toothache didn't seem very terrifying.

'Toothache for four hundred and fifty years! That can't be much fun,' said Mr Suttle.

'Nay, sir. That's why I magicked myself into nothingness.'

'Well now, look here,' said Chief Inspector Jethwa. 'You could have gone to the dentist, after all!'

Black William gave a little shriek.

'Dentists in his day were a bit terrifying,' Mr Suttle explained. 'Pincers, you know. Painful.'

Black William **nodded violently**.

'Well, my dentist is Miss Hodgkins in Blackbury and I never feel a thing, what with these modern anaesthetics. But first Mr William here would have to turn everything back to the twenty-first century.'

They explained to Black William that Miss Hodgkins was much better than the sort of tooth-blacksmiths of Elizabethan times. A sort of wizard for their age. And Black William agreed to remove his magic spell on the town as they travelled to see her.

Getting Black William into Blackbury was a very odd experience. Things changed back as they rode past. Stones became road signs again, trees turned back into telegraph poles, and a big grim forest changed once more into Blackbury Industrial Estate. In the town things began working again, sometimes with odd results, since washing machines and things had been left switched on or pushed into a corner.*

Miss Hodgkins's surgery was rather dirty and full of pincers until Black William reversed the spell,

when it suddenly became white and gleaming, with stainless-steel instruments in shiny trays. They explained to the dentist what had

---

* 'The Tale of the Rogue Carpet Sweeper' and 'My Narrow Escape from the Demon Lawn Mower' both became much-told future local legends as a result.

happened, and half an hour later Black William stepped from the chair with a lovely set of fillings.

"Tis a marvel!' he said, and waved a hand in the air. There was a shower of gold coins, rubies and emeralds in payment.

Then Black William vanished, with a smile on his face for the first time for over four centuries.

'Gone back to four hundred and fifty years ago,' said Mr Suttle. 'There go all the bright clothes and songs.'

'And the lack of hot water and medicine,' said Chief Inspector Jethwa. 'I can't say I'm sorry to see him go. Life is quite exciting enough as it is. Do you think I should get a shovel and collect up all these coins and jewels?'

'We could sell them, then spend the money to help clear up the mess,' agreed Mr Suttle.

'I wonder if he'll be back?' Chief Inspector

Jethwa said as he looked around for a broom.

Mr Suttle and Chief Inspector Jethwa never did see Black William again. But if you were ever to visit the Blackbury allotments in the thick of night, you might just sense a mysterious presence near Mr Suttle's cabbage patch . . . and hear a ghostly but contented munching sound if you listen very carefully.

THE FROZEN FEUD

You probably remember the story I told you some time ago about Llandanffwnfafegettupagogo, the little border town in the Wild West of England, and how PC Bryn Bunyan – the fastest truncheon west of the River Severn – caught the bandit Big Dai Evans.

Well, things were pretty quiet after that. But things never stay quiet for long in Wales.

One day Police Sergeant Bunyan – he had been promoted – was on traffic duty in the High Street, when PC Gorsebush Jones came running up.

'They're at it again, Sergeant! Fighting outside the post office!'

'I've had enough of this. Take over,' said Bunyan, and leaping upon his bicycle he pedalled off furiously down the road.

He turned the corner and frowned. On one side of the road was a large white ice-cream van with **MR FREEZY ICES** painted on the side in red letters.

Right in front of it was another van, painted red and pink, belonging to *Roof's Ice Cream*. Both were chiming away, and between them three ice-cream men were fighting.

'Hallo, 'allo, 'allo, what's all this then, break it up, break it up,' said Sergeant Bunyan. 'I've told

you before, any more of this and I'll run you in for breaching the peace.'

'This town ain't big enough for two ice-cream men,' said Mr Roof, aiming a blow at the others.

'Git out by sundown or we'll let your tyres down,' said Dafydd Freezy, who with his brother Herbert ran the second van. In Llandanff they were known as the Mr Freezy Brothers.

The trouble was that the town just could not keep both vans in business, and so every time they met there was usually a fight. Both said that they had been in business longest, and both thought the other was taking all the trade away.

Sergeant Bunyan got them to get into their vans and drive off in different directions, but he knew that he was going to have trouble with them again.

Next time they met they'd start throwing things, and Sergeant Bunyan wanted to keep the

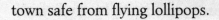

town safe from flying lollipops.

He was having a quiet afternoon game of dominoes with Gorsebush Jones when Tommy Taten the grocer rushed into the police station. There was a cornet stuck to the back of his head, and strawberry ice cream was running down his neck. Police Dog Blodwen leaped up to do her duty and lick it all off him.

Sergeant Bunyan picked up his truncheon, made sure his notebook was loaded, and said: 'Where are they this time?'

'Up-pupup at-tt-t Owen Kipp's sheep d-d-d-dip,' said Taten, his teeth chattering and sheepdog slobber now running down his neck.

Gorsebush brought the bikes out of the yard, and the two policemen pedalled off, leaving Blodwen in charge of the police station.

'I aim to clean up Llandanff,' said Bunyan, 'and that starts with ice cream on grocers.'

Soon they reached a big sign which said:

Everything was quiet. They put their bikes against the fence and crept up behind the water pump.

'Can you see anything yet, Sarge?'

'There's a Freezy van over there, but it's empty.'

Suddenly a Freezy's Iced Treat hit the pump above Gorsebush Jones's head and shattered.

'Dafydd Freezy's up on the roof of Taten's grocer's!'

The Freezy Brother was sitting on the roof with a big pile of ice creams by his side, and even

 as the policemen looked up he was taking aim with a Chocolate Family Block. But before he could throw it, a Roof's Custard Delight hit him between the eyes.

'Take that, you varmint!'

Mr Roof was shouting, dancing across the road before skipping smartly out of the way of a fusillade

of Choc 'n' Nut cones thrown his way by Herbert Freezy.

'Good shot, pardner!' Dafydd Freezy called down, only to duck as Mr Roof retaliated with a well-aimed Lemon Drizzle Tub.

'The Roof man is over behind the shed, Sarge,' Gorsebush reported. It was obvious to him that the Freezy Brothers had Mr Roof cornered.

But Mr Roof was fighting back. He suddenly rushed out, a handful of cornets in each hand.

'Ahoy, all of you! Enough of this!' shouted PC Gorsebush, but an iced lolly knocked his helmet off.

Quick as a flash, he grabbed the lolly and hurled it back up at Dafydd Freezy.

Soon the battle was in full swing again, and Sergeant Bunyan dashed over to the open Freezy van and came back with armfuls of Family Bricks.

As soon as the three ice-cream men saw what he had done they left their hiding places and came walking across the yard, ice creams in either hand.

The two policemen faced them.

'I'm taking you in for breach of the peace, obstruction and assaulting a police officer,' said Sergeant Bunyan.

'Hold it right there. Move your hands **reeeaaal slooow**,' Gorsebush drawled, lolly in his hand.

'Go for your ice cream!' replied Herbert Freezy.

Splat! Splat! Fast on the draw, faster than a speeding bullet, in one movement PC Jones hurled two Family Bricks, just as the Freezy Brothers were preparing to throw. The Bricks knocked both of them to the floor. A well-slung Raspberry Surprise from Mr Roof nearly caught him on the ear, but Sergeant Bunyan ran forward and dropped a cold lolly down the front of Mr

Roof's trousers and the ice-cream vendor sank to his knees, his face going a very funny colour.

Using a special judo hold he had been taught at Blackbury Police College, Sergeant Bunyan then marched his three prisoners to one of the vans, and he and PC Jones drove back into Llandanff.

'There's been altogether too much of this sort of thing,' said the Chairman of the Magistrates next day. 'I intend to make an example of you three. But Sergeant Bunyan had a suggestion to make, and if you do what he proposes and behave yourselves we'll say no more about this.'

So the very sorry ice-cream men went out and were made to paint their vans the same colours – red, white and blue. On both of them were painted the words:

Llandanff and District Ice Creams

Herbert Freezy drove one, Mr Roof drove the other, and Dafydd Freezy kept the books.

They made much more money because they weren't fighting, and it was peaceful in Llandanff once again – all thanks to Sergeant Bunyan and PC Jones.

DARBY AND
THE SUBMARINE

The pond was in the middle of a wood, surrounded by thickets of bramble and weeds. A small stream tumbled over a waterfall from it, and trickled away through the fields into the big river. It was a peaceful sort of place; no one ever came there.

On one bank, all twisted and gnarly with its roots sticking out in the brown water, was an old

willow tree. There were holes between its roots that you might think were made by water rats, until you saw the little boats half hidden in the shadows. There was a landing stage made out of splinters, about as long as your little finger, and even wicker pots for catching caddis-fly larvae, and fine nets hung up to dry.

On this particular day Darby was right out in the middle of the pond, rowing himself along in his walnut-shell boat and whistling. The other people who lived beneath the willow dared not go out as far, but here the duckweed grew thickly and the tadpoles swam in shoals. Tadpoles didn't taste very nice, but eating them was good for you.

'Quack!' went a duck, landing right by the boat and giving him a deeply menacing look.

Darby looked round, gulped, and dived for his life.

That was a long swim back to the willow! He only dared to come up for air when he was in some weeds, and all the time he could see the duck's feet paddling through the water above him.

He finally crawled onto the landing stage, dripping wet, and the people clustered around. There were all sorts: mothers, babies, granddads, uncles – all about a centimetre tall.

'It's the duck again,' **gasped** Darby. 'Nearly got me that time!'

'That means all our food will be scared away,' said Han the chieftain. 'Or eaten. Us too.'

The professor stepped forward, stroking his long white beard. 'I think this is the time to try our anti-duck device,' he said.

So the people ran down the long tunnels inside the willow until they came to a cavern. It was a hollow place inside the roots, and from it a narrow passage went out to the water.

A tiny submarine was tied to the wall. The professor opened the hatch and clambered inside, followed by Darby and the chieftain. Then they closed the hatch and opened the valves, and the submarine glided down into the dark water.

It came out from the roots into a fairyland of golden light, as the sunlight shimmered down through the brown water and shone from every sunken stone. The submarine was made out of a whole big walnut, and powered by an elastic band. It had taken Darby and the professor years

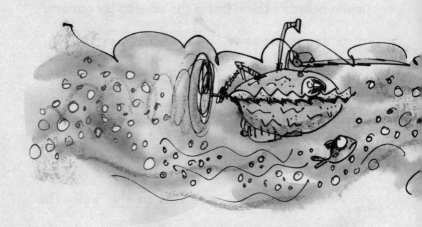

to build it, but it was a fine craft – it even had a working periscope and, instead of torpedoes, a long hawthorn spike fitted to its prow.

Slowly it drifted through the water, leaving a little trail of bubbles. Darby was looking through the periscope.

Then he saw the duck, which from underneath looked like a fat boat with legs.

'Duck ahead!' he cried. 'Stand by the ram! Full elastic!'

Han pulled back a lever and the submarine gathered speed.

The nasty duck didn't know what hit it. The tiny submarine shot up and rammed it amidships, and the bird whizzed out of the water with a quack. Back at the willow-tree landing stage all the people cheered.

Again the submarine headed for the duck. But it had had enough. Before the craft reached it, it was flying away over the reeds. It never came back. Not surprising, really.

In the walnut-shell sub, the professor, Han and Darby were so busy cheering and patting one another on the back that they didn't notice that the elastic-band motor had completely unwound itself. But the people on the shore did.

They were heading for the waterfall!

'Hey!' said Han. 'We seem to still be moving.'

'Right-ho, Professor, reverse engines,' said Darby, grasping the steering wheel.

'I can't! The elastic would have to be wound up again!'

Darby could hear a far-off roaring. **'Dive! It's our only chance!'**

The professor grabbed the little hand-pump

that worked the ballast tanks.

He was too late! The waterfall wasn't very big – just a trickle of water over some stones – but for people only a centimetre high, it was quite big enough. It led into a little stream. The sub shot over the falls, spun round rapidly in a whirlpool, rolled over twice, and plopped into the water. Then it began to drift with the current.

'I think I'm going to be very sick,' said the professor. He rolled under a bunk.

Han was clinging to the periscope column while Darby struggled with the wheel. 'Don't,' he said. 'Wind up the motor instead.'

'We'll never make any headway against this current,' muttered Han.

To the people back on the landing stage it looked like they were sailing towards unknown lands. In truth, the submarine was drifting between giant hawthorn trees, where mysterious creepers of old man's beard hung down as far as the water. Strange birds were singing in the trees.

The stream was higher than usual, and bits of driftwood and dead leaves were floating in it. In the middle of all this the tiny submarine spun slowly to the surface.

The hatch opened, and the professor and Darby

climbed out. On all sides there was nothing but water, and the waterfall was a long way behind them.

'Well, what are we going to do—' And as he said that, the professor slipped, and fell into the water with a *plop*.

'All right, all right, don't panic,' said Darby, and he dived in to pull him out – the old man couldn't swim very well, and he was already blowing bubbles.

As Darby surfaced and looked around he heard Han calling. The chieftain was jumping up and down and shouting at the top of his voice.

'Stickleback! Look out behind you! Stickleback!'

Darby turned, and could see a fin shooting through the water towards him. It was a spiny stickleback – the most feared fish in the stream!

Quickly he pushed the half-drowned professor onto a floating twig, and dived down. Underwater the light was yellow and dim, and he could hear a rushing noise in his ears. He put his knife of tough bramble-thorn between his teeth and looked about him for the stickleback.

It came rushing at him with its fearsome jaws open, and he ducked just in time. Then it turned for another attack, and Darby plunged his thorn-knife into its belly. It was a bitter struggle, and the water turned red with stickleback blood, as the fish thrashed around trying to get Darby between its long teeth. He felt as though his head would burst: it was such a long time since he had taken a breath.

Up on the surface Han pulled the professor onto the submarine and watched the churning water anxiously. Just when he was about to give up Darby clambered aboard.

'Quick! Wind up the motor, there might be more of them about!'

The submarine went on down the stream. It had portholes, and the adventurers looked through at a strange underwater world.

Tadpoles and water beetles swam up and peered in at them, and the three adventurers had their lunch while the creatures swam around the sub.

The stream went under a small bridge and wound out into the river, and the little submarine whirled out into the current.

'I say,' said Han, pushing his plate away. 'The stream seems to have got bigger all of a sudden.'

'Yes, it has,' said Darby. 'Up periscope!'

'Hey, the bank looks a long way away,' he said after a while, 'and there's a great big—

'Dive, quickly!'

The others grabbed the pumps and pulled with all their might. Overhead came the sound of powerful engines, and the water foamed.

'What on earth was it?' said the professor, after the noise had gone.

'I'm not sure – it looked like a giant boat. Nearly hit us too. Stay submerged for a while. You never know.'

The water was muddy, and they could see nothing outside.

'Well, how are we going to get out of this mess?' asked Han.

'I'm more concerned with staying alive, quite frankly,' said Darby. 'Anyway, how about we play a game of dominoes?'

*

After a while the professor raised the periscope again. 'Can you hear anything?' he said. 'Like a sort of faraway rushing?'

There was a sudden gurgling noise and a roar, and the lights of the sub were reflected off nearby walls. They were in a pipe!

The current swept them along faster and faster, round bends and through thrashing pumps – *bang! bang! bang!* went the big engines of the waterworks (for that was what it was), and the tiny craft was bowled over and over and sent rushing along smaller and smaller pipes.

With a thud the submarine wedged in the pipe, upside down. The water trickled underneath it.

'I think we ought to abandon ship,' said Darby, 'mainly because there is a big crack opening in the wall.'

They all stared at it.

Darby wrenched a pipe out of the wall and fiddled with it. 'If you tie this to your head and make a funnel here so that it fits over your mouth, I think you'll have a good snorkel tube,' he said. Then he waited until the professor and Han had made one for themselves, and opened the hatch.

The light glimmered on the damp walls of a long dark tunnel that stretched upwards; there was a tiny point of light at the far end. In the distance he could hear rumblings and bangings.

Unknown to him, Mr Arnold Grapeshot was banging on the cold water tap, and wondering why the water had stopped coming out. 'Have to send for the plumber,' he muttered. He wrapped a towel around himself and dripped his way downstairs.

As the door closed a very small head looked out of the tap.

'Well I never!' gasped Darby. He was looking out at a gigantic porcelain valley filled with soapy water, and half hidden in the steam a copper geyser rumbled like a volcano. A floating loofah looked bigger than a whale to him, and a soap dish seemed like a mountain.

'This looks the sort of place where you get giants,' said the professor in a matter-of-fact voice.

'Lost in the plumbing,' said Han.

'I say! Look at that!' cried Darby. On the far end of the bath lay a boat, a big clockwork one with a red hull. 'What a magnificent machine! Do you think we could reach it?'

'But why?' grumbled Han. 'This pond is too small, and there's no way out.'

'Yes, but that's exactly the sort of boat that giants sometimes sail on our pond,' said Darby. 'Remember? We always have to hide.'

Taking a deep breath, he made a beautiful swallow dive and disappeared in the soapy water. Han followed him more slowly, towing the professor carefully behind him.

It took a long time to swim to the other side of the bath, and climbing the slippery side took a lot of effort. But tiny hands and feet found holds in the porcelain.

'Hey, this is not at all bad,' said Han, when they had all climbed into the boat. 'Look, a motor and sails. And a rudder. Funny sort of motor, though.'

'I think you have to wind it up,' the professor said.

'Well, I suppose we'll just have to sit here and wait,' said Darby. 'I don't suppose there's anything to eat?'

'I saw some spiders' webs on the ceiling,' said Han.

'Well, we'll see what we can find later. In the meantime I'm going to get a bit of kip,' said Darby.

'We're being picked up!' cried Han.

'About time,' muttered Darby. 'I'm getting fed up with this.'

The three of them had been living in the toy boat on the bathroom shelf for several days, living on earwigs and other insects that dropped into the bath. They didn't taste very nice, but there you are.* The professor had spent his time examining the clockwork motor.

They clung to the sides as the boat was picked up and dumped into a giant bag, with towels and bathing costumes.

'Now here's the plan,' said Darby, as they

* An earwig will actually make a lot of meals if you are only one centimetre high.

bumped along. 'As soon as the boat is put in the water I want you, Han, to grab the tiller. Professor, can you work the motor?'

'It'll need winding up every now and then.'

'Yes, well, if possible we'll abandon this one and find a better boat.'

Hours later, a giant hand reached down and wound up the motor, then put the boat into a pond. **'Right!'** cried Darby. **'Everyone to action stations.'**

Han grabbed the tiller and wrenched it round so that the boat **whizzed** out into the middle of the boating pool. The little boy who owned it looked on in amazement.

'Hmm, this is fresh water,' said Darby, looking over the side. 'It must come in somewhere. Hey, look at that!' *That* was a big electric-driven boat that dwarfed their own.

'What a craft!' said the professor. 'Think we can board her, Darby?' He brought the boat up alongside it.

'We'll try,' said Darby. 'Follow me.' He leaped across, climbed up the side of the model and peered into the bridge. A couple of big switches were screwed into the floor. 'This looks pretty easy to operate,' he said. **'All aboard!'** He threw down a rope and the others scrambled across to join in.

The big model shot across the pond towards the water inlet tunnel while Darby struggled with the tiller. Then it was through and out onto the river, shooting along and leaving a trail of foam behind it. **'Hold tight!'** Darby shouted as they narrowly missed a swan. 'And look out for the stream!'

'There's an opening over there!'

Darby pulled hard on the tiller and the boat skimmed across the river and up the stream. A few minutes later it buried its nose in the bank by the waterfall.

'Ah, back home at last,' the professor sighed with relief. 'I hope I never have another ride like that in my life.'

They waded out and began to climb up the stones around the waterfall.

'You know,' said Darby thoughtfully, 'with a proper crew I'm sure we could have a lot of fun with that boat. I don't think there is anything more grand than messing about on the water.'

'You are right,' said the professor. 'Three men in a boat!'

THE SHEEP RODEO SCANDAL

I've told you before about Llandanffwnfafeget-tupagogo, the most lawless town in the real Wild West – that is, Wales. This is what happened there one year at the Annual Sheep Rodeo and Dog Trials.

It was a Friday night and Police Sergeant Bryn Bunyan – the fastest truncheon west of the border –

was having supper with his friends PC Gorsebush Jones and Doc Rees when the High Street was suddenly full of shouting.

Gorsebush opened the door, then slammed it again as half a dozen sheep tried to get into the room.

'It's the sheepboys in town again,' he said. 'They only come once a year, but once is enough. They've just got paid too, by the sound of it.'

Every year the sheepboys drove the flocks down from the mountain to sell them at the Sheep Rodeo, and that always meant trouble, what with people getting in brawls and staying up as late as midnight.

'I think I'll just mosey on down to the pub,' said Sergeant Bunyan.

'I think I'll mosey with you,' said Doc Rees. 'There's bound to be a few cracked heads once those boys taste a bit of brown ale.'

When they reached the Lump o' Coke people were singing. Someone was playing the piano and everyone else was shouting and banging on the bar.

The two friends stood outside for a few minutes, sniffing the evening air, and then there was a mighty

CRASH!

as someone was thrown through the window. They lay motionless on the pavement.

'It's Woolley Waistcoat,' said Doc. 'Hmm. No bones broken,' he added, with obvious disappointment.

'Isn't he the boss of the Lazy Z farm?'

'Yep.'

Next moment the door burst open and a stream of sheepboys poured out onto the pavement, fighting. Sergeant Bunyan thought for a moment, then blew his police whistle – hard.

PEEEEEEEEP!

Everyone stopped as if by magic.

Sergeant Bunyan flexed his knees.

'Evenin' all, and hullo, hullo, what's all this?' he said. 'In town five minutes and already causing a Breach of the Peace? That's quick work.'

'You ask that sheep-thief Waistcoat,' said a tall thin man who Bunyan recognized as Rawhide Evans, who owned the Sulky Leek farm.

'It's him that's been stealing sheep!' said Woolley Waistcoat, pointing at Evans.

'I see. You want to lay charges of sheep stealing against each other, eh?'

'Yes,' they said together.

'I can prove that he's been rustling my sheep,' they said at the same time, then scowled at each other.

The two farms were next to each other, up in

the hills at the end of the valley. Waistcoat and Evans normally got on quite well, whispered Doc. Something was up.

'I'll have a word with you both in the morning,' said Bunyan. 'In the meantime, as I think I've said before, I aim to clean up this here town – and that means no fighting in the street . . .'

'If you ask me,' said Doc Rees, 'someone has been rustling sheep from Waistcoat and Evans and making each believe it's the other.'

'I suppose I could put one of them in jail for the night, for fighting,' said Sergeant Bunyan. 'But that wouldn't be fair. If I locked them both up they'd fight in the cell. The town's full up because of the Sheep Rodeo, and I don't want trouble.'

They were having breakfast in Auntie Megan's

Lucky Strike tea rooms. Gorsebush was busy trying to arrange his cooked breakfast into a smiley face on his plate.

'I'll tell you another thing,' said Doc, slurping his tea, 'the rustler is in town now. He's got to sell the sheep, hasn't he? And I shouldn't think he would risk taking them too far.'

At that moment someone strolled past the window. It certainly wasn't one of the Llandanff-wnfafegettupagogo residents. He wore a shiny top hat, a spotted bow tie and a fancy knitted waistcoat embroidered with red dragons. He had a droopy moustache and eyes hidden under two bushy eyebrows.

Sergeant Bunyan stared at him and slowly put down his fork. 'Do you know who that is?' he said.

'Just some city slicker from Cardiff, probably,' said Gorsebush, glancing up from his sausages.

'That's Maverock Weedon, the gambler. Half the pubs in Wales won't serve him. There's not a game he doesn't play – darts, dominoes, bar billiards, shove ha'penny – and he cheats at all of them. He might just be in town to win a bit of money, or he might be involved in this sheep stealing. Ah look, here he comes now.'

'G'd morning, gentlemen. Nice day, isn't it?' said Maverock Weedon as he sauntered over to the table, touching the brim of his top hat with one finger.

'That's right,' said Sergeant Bunyan. He lowered his voice. 'One marked domino and you'll be in trouble.'

'I wouldn't use language like that to a perfectly respectable citizen if I was you,' said Maverock sternly. 'As a matter of fact I've gone into the sheep-selling business.'

'I kind of thought you might have,' said Sergeant Bunyan. 'Whose sheep?'

'Mine, of course.' Maverock grinned. 'Two hundred of them. They're penned in at the O.K. Sheep Dip if you want to see them. It's all legal.' He lit a cigar and strolled away.

Sergeant Bunyan turned to his companions and raised his eyebrows. 'He's a wolf in sheep's clothing, you mark my words.'

Later Sergeant Bunyan and PC Gorsebush Jones went to the Sheep Dip. There were the Waistcoat sheep, marked with a cross, and the Evans sheep, marked with a circle. The Maverock flock was penned between them, each sheep marked with a cross inside a circle.

'It'd be easy to turn those markings into the Maverock mark,' said Gorsebush, 'and I've seen

that Maverock with young Dai Too, who's aimin' to step into his brother's boots now Big Dai's in jail.* They're just the sort to rustle sheep.'

'But we can't prove it,' said Sergeant Bunyan. 'The rodeo starts tomorrow. He'll sell the sheep then and disappear. I could check in town that he does own them, check that brand of his out, but it would take too long.'

'Then you're stuck,' said Gorsebush.

'But we've got to stop him selling the sheep tomorrow,' said Sergeant Bunyan.

'How about stealing them?' said Gorsebush. 'My dog Blodwen'll round them up tonight.'

'That's illegal,' said Sergeant Bunyan sternly. 'In other words, don't let me catch you doing it.'

That night Maverock Weedon's sheep – which had really been rustled from two other sheep

* Not that easy, since Dai Too's feet were two sizes smaller than Big Dai's, so he had to wear three pairs of socks.

farms – disappeared from their pen, then at dawn Gorsebush Jones cycled madly to town to find out if Maverock really owned the sheep.

I wonder where Jones has hidden the sheep? wondered Sergeant Bunyan when Maverock stormed into the police station to complain.

'It's a busy day today, you know,' he said. 'The Sheep Rodeo is on, but I'll see what I can do.'

'I want them back!' shouted Maverock. 'I've got to sell them today.'

'I don't expect they have been taken far,' said Sergeant Bunyan.

No sooner had Maverock left than Sergeant Bunyan heard a sound from the cells behind the station. He opened the spyhole and shut it again quickly. The cells were full of sheep, and there was a note pinned to the door. It said:

Dere Sir. I dint kno where ells to put them.
Yores Fafethully,
G. Jones

Outside, the Sheep Rodeo was in full swing, with sheep-dip competitions, sheepdog trials and shearing races all going on at the same time. Through the middle of all this came Gorsebush, pedalling furiously.

He dashed into the police station waving a piece of paper.

'There's no such brand as the one Maverock's got on the sheep,' he cried. **'It's a forgery! Those sheep are stolen!'**

Bunyan clapped his helmet on his head. 'Right,' he said.

He opened the door – and a pair of sheep shears thudded into the post by his ear.

Then Dai Too, who had been listening at the window, leaped onto Gorsebush's bike and sped away, with Maverock – who had hurled the shears – perched on the crossbar.

'Stop those men!'

bellowed Sergeant Bunyan. 'They're going to be in Llandanffwnfafegettupagogo Magistrates Court on Monday!'

'They pinched sheep!' added Gorsebush, peering round the door. All the sheepboys turned

and sprinted up the street.

'Now that isn't quite correct,' said Sergeant Bunyan, turning to Gorsebush. 'They're not officially guilty until Monday. That's the law, you see – everyone's innocent until found guilty.

'STOP THOSE SNEAKY SHEEP RUSTLERS!' he added.

The street was now empty except for Alun Allen the milkman, who was trotting along on his milk cart. Sergeant Bunyan leaped aboard, shouted, **'Giddyup!'** snatched the reins, and the milk cart disappeared after the sheepboys.

'We'll never catch up with them now,' moaned Gorsebush, as the milk cart rumbled into the hills.

Sergeant Bunyan slowed the milkman's horse to a walk. 'You're quite right,' he said. 'This needs thinking about.'

It was peaceful in the hills above Llandanff-wnfafegettupagogo. The birds were singing, bees were zooming like tiny fighter planes in the heather, and the horse stopped to crop the grass.

Sergeant Bunyan removed his helmet and mopped his brow. Suddenly he sat up straight. 'I know – we'll head them off at Plimsoll's Yat,' he said.

Now Plimsoll's Yat was where the road out of Llandanff etc. ran along a line of wooded hills overlooking the River Severn. The Yat itself was a shelf of rock that stuck out a couple of hundred metres over the river.*

Up in the hills Dai Too the sheep rustler and the gambler Maverock had lost the posse of sheep-boys, and were freewheeling down the long slope that led to the Yat.

'Isn't that a milk cart in the road down there?' asked Maverock, peering over Dai's shoulder.

'Yes,' growled Dai, and put the brakes on. Now the fact was that he was riding Gorsebush's bike, which Gorsebush used to stop by ramming his boots onto the front wheel. To put it another way, it had no brakes.

* One day a man called Plimsoll had fallen off it, so people thought the least they could do was name it after him.

The wheels were turning so fast they were a blur. Sergeant Bunyan and Gorsebush peered from behind the cart with horror as the bike, with two screaming people on it, whirred towards them.

With a *twang* it hit a stone and shot off sideways, through a hedge, across a stream in a shower of spray, through another hedge, over a tree root, through a small wood . . . and up into the air like a bird.

It sailed over the Yat and started the long fall into the river. When Sergeant Bunyan and Gorsebush got to the edge, all they could see was a widening pool of ripples a long way below, with Maverock's shiny top hat floating in the centre. Gorsebush snatched his own hat off and stood, looking sad.

'Oi!' came a voice from halfway up a hawthorn tree, just behind them. It was Maverock, wedged into the brambles. And they found Dai Too lying in the hedge, looking puzzled – *and* bootless, since his boots had got stuck in the bicycle wheel, and he had lost both boots and two pairs of socks. Both were so dazed that they just sat quietly in the milk cart while it trundled back to town.

'Here,' said Gorsebush. **'We can't put them in the cells! The police station's full of sheep!'**

'Those sheep are going to be needed on Monday as evidence,' said Sergeant Bunyan. 'I'm afraid Dai and Maverock will just have to stay in there with them.'

And so they did.

But first all the sheepboys had to come and offer for the sheep which were, of course, still for sale. And how they laughed to see the sheep rustlers in the same pen as the sheep.

'I'll gi' ye ten pounds for that critter there!' Woolley Waistcoat chortled, pointing at the

bootless Dai Too, who was struggling to hang onto his last pair of socks while a persistent ewe tried to eat them.

'An' I'll see ye the same for that one over there wi' a chewed waistcoat wrapped around his skinny self,' Rawhide Evans offered back, pointing at a decidedly sheepish-looking Maverock.

And all the sheepboys cheered.

AN ANT CALLED 4179003

Once or twice upon a time there was an ant called 4179003. He lived in an ants' nest with a lot of other ants who all looked alike. He didn't even have any friends, because ant number 4179004, with whom he had been quite friendly, had one day got trodden on by a dog. In the ants' nest it was dark and every day was just like yesterday.

Then one day 4179003 was lumping around ants' eggs with all the other ants and he thought: Why am I doing this? Is this what life is all about?

He stopped for a moment and put down his load.

That's a subversive thought, he thought, shocked at himself. If the Queen finds out I'll be executed and my number will be given to a new ant. I'm not being loyal to the nest.

He heaved the ants' eggs a bit further down the tunnel.

Yesterday I was carrying eggs and I'll be carrying eggs tomorrow, he thought. It didn't seem a very exciting prospect. The more he thought about it the less exciting it became.

So blow this for a lark, thought 4179003 finally, dropping his eggs and trotting towards the entrance.

*

It didn't take long for his disappearance to be noticed. One of the soldier ants, the ones with great clicking jaws, was watching the column wind by when he noticed the gap in it. Immediately he gave the alarm.

'A defector!' he screamed. 'Stop him!'

But it was too late: 4179003 had gone.

He was running through the grass stems, peering constantly over his shoulder. It was a good job he did. Soldier ants were swarming out of the nest, jaws clashing in fury.

He bumped into a blade of grass, and for want of anything else to do sped up it. It shook as the soldiers tramped by.

'Hmm,' said a voice from right behind him.

'Gah!' said 4179003, spinning round. A large grasshopper was watching him, and then it peered over the edge of the blade.

'They're going to a lot of trouble over one ant,' it said. 'Done something nasty, have you? Hmmm?'

'It is forbidden to leave the nest without permission,' quavered 4179003.

'Oh, I won't turn you in,' said the grasshopper. 'We're all open-minded here, I'm sure. What's your name?'

'They call me Ant 4179003.'

'That's a number! I mean, what do you call yourself?'

'Just me,' said 4179003.

'Well, Me's good enough,' muttered the grasshopper. 'You've got to have a name. Still, once an ant always an ant. I knew a bee once that felt the same as you. Wanted to see a bit more of the world.

Didn't work. Got hungry. Got cold. Fed up. No, the likes of you ought to stick in nests. Nip in quick before the soldiers come back and I dare say no one'll notice you've been away.'

'No! I want to see what's going on!' said Me.

The grasshopper eyed him carefully. 'Another reason you ought to get back in is that sometimes when I'm hungry I eat ants. No offence meant, I'm sure – it's just in my nature. I mean, if I was to get hungry in the next few minutes I might feel called upon to eat you.'

Me backed away and slid back down the grass stem.

'You'll regret it,' sang the grasshopper from his perch. But Me scurried off through the grass.

At last he crawled up onto a dock leaf and looked around. There was no sign of the soldier ants who had been chasing him, or of the grasshopper.

Free! he thought, doing a little jig on the leaf. No more numbers! No more being bossed around. Whoopee!

The sun was shining and he felt marvellous. He cartwheeled across the leaf and did all those things he wasn't allowed to do in the hive – somersaults, whistling and stamping all six feet. After about five minutes of this he'd run out of things to do and was getting hungry.

Honey, he thought. There must be some way of getting the stuff without going back to the nest. To tell the truth, he had never bothered about where food came from – he'd just queued up in the ants' canteen, like everyone else.

Just then there was a buzzing above him. It stopped, there was a cough, and it started again. This happened several times, and then there was a crash and a bee bounced off the dock leaf, cursing.

The ant peered over the edge. 'Are you hurt?'

'Only my pride, laddie, only my pride,' said the bee from where he was lying. 'Engine's conked out. Have to walk home now. Are you this ant I'm supposed to be looking for?'

It dawned on the ant. 'You must be the bee the grasshopper mentioned, the one who left the hive.'

'That's me. Thought I'd look you up, y'know. We rebels must stick together. I say, I'd be obliged if you could help me up.'

The ant levered the bee up with a grass stem, and helped him smooth out his wings.

'That's better,' said the bee. 'Name's Bottomly. H'd y'do? Fancy a walk? Got a little place up under the hedge. Nothing flash, but homely. Expect you're hungry. Got honey. Come on.' And he crawled away, with the ant running to keep up.

As they progressed, Bottomly explained, in brief sentences, how he'd got fed up with living in the hive and had decided to run away.

'That's exactly what I thought too,' said the ant admiringly. 'I got fed up with doing the same things every day.'

'Too true, laddie. Where's it all lead to? I asked myself. Nowhere. So I've got this deserted mouse hole, which is quite cosy. Sometimes I see a few old friends from the hive, but they've never got time to talk. Work, work, work, that's all they care about.'

He led the ant up a bank and into the hole. It was small and warm inside, and the walls were lined with honey pots. Bottomly prised the lid off one and offered the ant a drink.

'Cheers,' he said.

'Cheers,' said the ant. It looked as though freedom wasn't going to be too bad after all.

They were just starting on a second pot of honey when Bottomly glanced out of the mouse hole.

'Here come those soldier ants!' he cried. 'They've followed us!'

The ant peered out and saw them marching up the bank. There were *hundreds* of them. He could hear their jaws clicking, their feet stamping out a tune, which they were chanting as they climbed:

'Us ants go marching left and right,

Hurrah, hurrah,

Ten thousand legs is quite a sight,

Hurrah, hurrah!

We work all day

'Cos that's our way

And we all go marching on . . .'*

'You don't weigh much,' said Bottomly, picking Me up. 'Hold on – I'm going to try to take off.'

With his wings going like buzz saws the bee bumped and bounced down the slope, and soared into the evening air just above the snapping jaws of the soldiers.

The ant looked dizzily down and saw the soldier ants invading the mouse hole.

'They'll eat all your honey!' he said. 'Oh, I'm sorry.'

'Never mind about that. I can't fly far with you, so we'd better look for a landing spot. Fasten your seat belts and no smoking please.' He swallowed. 'You seem to have got heavier.'

Me looked round – and saw a soldier ant hanging onto Bottomly's back legs.

* They were good soldiers, but not very good at making up songs. I expect you could make up a better one.

'We've been boarded!' he shouted.

'This is a hijack,' said the soldier ant. 'Fly to the
ant heap, or I'll bite.' He clashed his jaws.

Bottomly soared upwards and somersaulted.
He spiralled and buzzed across the sky, with both
ants clinging on tightly.

'No tricks—' began the soldier, but just then Me leaped at him and grabbed his legs, pulling him off Bottomly.

They tumbled down, with the bee a tiny speck above them. The soldier, being heavier, fell faster, and the small ant was left alone, slowly floating in the breeze.

There was a whirr of wings and Bottomly soared down and hovered under him. 'Climb aboard,' he said.

They swooped across a wood and Bottomly hovered over a stream.

'Hold tight,' he called. 'I can't go on much longer.'

They landed in a clump of watercress, and sat panting on the broad damp leaves.

'This looks a nice place,' said the ant, as they scrambled up the bank. 'Homely. And a nice long way from the ants' nest.'

'That looks an interesting hole over there,' said the bee.

The hole had belonged to a rat, but was now deserted except for an earwig, who scuttled away as they approached.

'Room for lots of honey here,' said Bottomly. 'Roomy sort of place. Nice view of the water. Peaceful.'

And there they stayed, doing nothing at all most days but gathering a bit of honey and watching the stream go by, while the other ants and bees worked hard and never had time to watch anything.

THE FIRE OPAL

Long before there were men on Earth there was a mountain so high that its top was forever hidden in the clouds. It was called Whitehelm, and at its tip, in a tiny hollow in the black rock, was a peaceful valley.

There the mountain people lived. Trolls, they were called. They were half as tall as houses, and their skins were harder than stone.

Their king had a crown of iron and lead. In its centre was the Fire Opal.

The Fire Opal came from the centre of the Earth. It shone with all colours, even at night, when the clouds around the mountain reflected the glow. The trolls said that their ancestors had brought it with them when they came up from the centre of the Earth.

One day the old king crumbled away as old rock falls into dust, and the new prince was to be crowned. His name was Tyran Ogg.

He didn't particularly want to be a king – he wanted to lead an expedition to explore the lands down below the mountain.

To tell the truth, he was bored with the valley too. He wanted to go to the moon. He used to look up at it on clear nights and wish he was there, because it was bleak and rocky, the kind of place that trolls love. And of course, as trolls were half stone, they could talk to rocks and mountains, so he felt sure that it would be wonderful to have a chat with the moon.

If only we could go there, he thought.

Then, just as the archbishop troll was placing the crown on his head, the Fire Opal fell out with a *plop!* and started to roll down the valley.

'Quick! Stop it!' cried the archbishop, and the prince and his soldiers dashed after it. It bounced and rolled and, at the very edge of the valley, stopped.

'Don't nobody breathe,' said the Sergeant of the Guard, tiptoeing towards it. He reached out – and next moment all they saw were his toes, swinging on the edge. Ogbuff, the palace cook, jumped forward and grabbed at the guard's ankles.

Prince Tyran Ogg caught the cook's collar. Then the edge, with three weighty trolls on it, gave way. Those who dared to look saw three figures getting smaller and smaller until they disappeared into the clouds, with the Fire Opal glittering among them.

'They'll be killed!' said someone.

'No,' said the archbishop. 'Trolls can stand anything. But I don't think they'll be able to get up again. The Fire Opal will go on rolling until it reaches the centre of the Earth, where it came from.'

Down through the clouds tumbled the trolls. Ogbuff saw the ground coming towards him uncomfortably fast.

Thud! Bonk! Crash!

The three trolls bounced and tumbled through the pine woods beneath Whitehelm Mountain, smashing trees and leaving large dents in the ground. Luckily, trolls are almost indestructible, so Prince Tyran only had a slight headache when he reached the bottom and crawled out of the crater he had made.

His crown of iron and lead had been knocked

over his eyes, and he stumbled around for a while, wrenching at it. Then he found the Sergeant of the Guard hanging by his heels from a tall tree.

They discovered Ogbuff, the cook, sitting up to his ears in a pond, blowing bubbles.

But no one found the Fire Opal.

'I thought it bounced over that way,' said the sergeant, pointing towards a thick forest. They were still quite high up, and the countryside was spread out like a map before them.

Prince Tyran peered up through the clouds around Whitehelm and shivered. 'Now we're here we'd better go after it,' he said. 'I don't think a troll has been this far down since we came from the centre of the Earth. Come on.'

They tramped gloomily through the dark wood, three shadows against the trees. Their great heavy feet boomed like drums.

Boom!
Boom!
Boom!

It started to grow dark, and a big orange moon rose above the forest. The prince gazed up at it, his dreams still filling his head.

Ogbuff was the last in the line, trying to look all ways at once. After a while he began to hear things. There were the trolls' footfalls – and something else.

Tramp, tramp, tramp. Tramp, tramp, tramp, thud! Tramp, tramp, tramp, tramp, thud! Thud!

'Argh!' he cried and cannoned forward into the sergeant, who tripped up and fell onto Prince Tyran. 'There's something behind us!'

'Good evening!' said a voice that seemed to come from very high up.

The prince peered up and saw a tall shape. It looked very much like a pine tree, until he got used to the light and saw that what he thought were pine needles were really whiskers around a gnarled face. 'Don't you know your history?' he said to Ogbuff, who was trying to burrow in the leaf mould. 'It's a wood troll, a dryad. They're practically related to us.'

'I'm sorry I startled your fat friend,' said the dryad in a voice like branches creaking in a high wind. 'My name is Arcantrellhyrodollomenemon. I saw you land.'

'We didn't see you,' said Tyran. 'I'm Tyran, Prince of Whitehelm, and this is Ogbuff, and this is the Sergeant of the Guard.'

'I know the sergeant,' said the dryad. 'He landed

upside down in my beard. You thought I was a tree, I think. Are you by any chance looking for a large shiny object?'

'Yes!' said Tyran. 'Have you found it?'

'A large shiny thing dropped through my roof just before you landed,' said the dryad. 'We can't have this, you know, damaging people's property . . .'

'It's the Fire Opal from my crown,' said Tyran. 'Have you still got it?'

The dryad scratched his beard with a noise like distant thunder. 'Well now,' he said. 'A funny thing, it bounced out of the door and rolled down the valley.'

'Which way? Which way!'

chorused the trolls.

The dryad pointed, and as they hurried off they heard him call: 'Don't damage any trees! I'll tell my relatives down the valley to look out for you!'

'What's he worried about trees for?' puffed Ogbuff, as they pounded over the pine needles.

'He's half a tree himself,' said Prince Tyran. 'The dryads herd trees like cattle, and they can talk to them, like we talk to rocks.'

As the three trolls hurried after the Opal, creaking noises sounded from the forest around them, and once or twice they saw eyes high up in the trees. The dryads were taking no chances of having their precious trees harmed.

Eventually they came to a place where two paths crossed. 'I wonder which way it went,' said Tyran.

What looked like a perfectly ordinary tree stretched out a branch to point, and said, **That way!**

'Thank you!' said the prince.

They were very glad to get out of the forest just as the sun was rising. Ahead of them were soggy green meadows, pierced with tall rushes, and in the middle of the valley was a wide brown river.

'I say, you people!' bellowed a voice from out in the middle of the water.

'It's a water nymph,' said Tyran.

'Um,' said the sergeant. 'I always thought they were – well, girls, with long hair and that sort of thing.'*

Indeed, the nymph was nothing like that. His head and shoulders and beard were all rush green, and he held a stem of mace in one hand. In the other was a fish, which he bashed around in the water to attract their attention.

'You stone people!' he bellowed. *'Come here!'*

Tyran and the others splashed out to the nymph. He smelled of river banks.

'Are you looking for a large shiny pebble?' he said.

---

* A bit sadly. He had especially been wondering what 'that sort of thing' might mean.

'That shiny pebble is really our Fire Opal,' said Prince Tyran. 'Have you got it?'

'It bounced straight into my private pool, nearly knocking me over,' said the nymph angrily. 'I don't know where it is now – it rolled on down the river, I suppose.'

'Look, it's very important to us,' explained Tyran. 'We've been following it all day. It's our Crown Jewel, you see.'

'In that case I might be able to find it,' said the nymph. He squinted at them. 'I suppose you're the kind of people who have to breathe air all the time?'

'We're stone trolls,' said Tyran proudly. 'We can hold our breaths under molten rocks if necessary.'

'Hmph,' said the nymph and dived, shouting,

'Follow me!'

Tyran, Ogbuff and the sergeant tramped along

the river bed after the nymph – trolls can't swim, they're much too heavy.

The water nymph told them he was in fact Icon, the king of the river. Every now and again he stopped to speak to the fish which swam around him like an army. The water was chilly and full of these fish, which swam round and round the trolls with uncomfortably hungry expressions.

'This river must be our own Trollwash,' said the sergeant in a cloud of bubbles, and they all thought of the little stream that ran out of the mountain.

When Icon finally swam up to the surface again the trolls all tramped up the bank until their heads poked out of the water like rocks.

'The current's rolling it on down to the sea,' said Icon. 'Was it very valuable?'

They all nodded gloomily.

'It's very big, the sea,' said Icon. 'It goes all around

the world. There's caves at the bottom of it, deeper than that mountain you live on.' He saw their glum expressions. 'Look here,' he added quickly, for he was a kindly soul, 'I've got a friend who lives in the sea, salty sort but nice chap. Sea troll, you know. Tell you what, we'll go and see him.'

All that day the trolls followed the river king down his river until the water got saltier and saltier, and the fish got bigger and the surface above them got greener.

'I can't come any further because of the salt,' said Icon. 'But just you walk ashore and I'll call him.'

The trolls clomped onto a lonely beach, noisy with surf and seagulls. Icon put his hands together and gave a long deep call. Nothing happened for a while, and then something started happening in the sea.

The sea bubbled and hissed, and suddenly, with a snort that silenced the seagulls, a large sad head bobbed up. It was blue and covered in scales, with a crown of brown seaweed tilted over one ear.

Icon cupped his hands together and called: 'These stone trolls are looking for their Fire Opal. Have you seen it?'

The head nodded.

'Off you go,' **hissed** Icon. 'He doesn't say much but he's a decent chap at heart.'

The trolls said their thank-yous to Icon, then waded awkwardly out through the surf until it closed over their heads. You might think it is quiet under the sea, but it is very noisy; they heard the roar of the tide, and the clanging of bells in drowned churches far away, the swirl of water over rock, and the sound of fish.

The sea troll swam slowly towards them. 'Come with me!' he boomed, in a cloud of bubbles.

'It's rotten cold,' said Ogbuff, shivering. 'And wet,' he added.

'My feet ache,' moaned the sergeant.

'Not far,' said the sea troll.

He led them down past sunken wrecks and goggle-eyed fish, while the water around them got greener and greener. Finally he stopped at a deep crevasse in the sea bed.

'Went down there,' he bubbled, then he blinked

slowly at them and started to swim away.

'Hey!' said Prince Tyran, but he was gone.

'It's dark down there,' said the sergeant dubiously.

'Deadly dangerous – probably octopuses, you know, and sharks,' added Ogbuff.

'Cowards!' said Tyran, and jumped into the crevasse. He sank for a long time, past dark fish with lights on their snouts and luminous teeth, until he landed with a slight bump on a round rock. He groped around in the dark, there was a slight *click!* and the dark shadows were lit by a blue glow.

It was the Fire Opal!

Prince Tyran had landed on one of the giant oysters that live in the deeps, and it had swallowed the Opal. He could see it inside the gaping shell, next to a big pearl.

Ogbuff and the sergeant floated slowly down into the glow.

'We thought we'd have to follow to make sure you weren't being eaten by sharks,' explained Ogbuff.

'Look at this!' said Tyran. The trolls clustered round the oyster and stared. Within the shell, the beautiful gemstone shone with a translucent splendour that seemed to reflect the beauty of the sea around it. By its side the pearl looked almost dull.

'You know, I think it's still trying to get to the centre of the Earth . . .' began Ogbuff, but Tyran wasn't listening.

He reached carefully into the oyster and grabbed the Opal. But he nudged the pearl – and there was a *snap!* and the Opal went flying out of the shell and rolled away behind some rocks. Tyran's arm was caught in the shell, but the skin of a stone troll is very hard and strong, and after he thumped

the oyster a couple of times it let go. After all, he hadn't been trying to take its pearl away so the oyster didn't mind too much.

Meanwhile Ogbuff had followed the Opal behind the rocks. He found a cave there. It led downwards.

'My feet really do ache,' moaned the sergeant.

The Fire Opal rolled on down through one cave after another with the three trolls in hot pursuit. They bounced down great tunnels and leaped rivers of molten lava, scurried through caverns glittering with diamonds and garnets – and all the time the Fire Opal was just out of reach, tumbling

steadily onwards to the centre of the Earth.

Ogbuff was puffing along behind the other two when they suddenly disappeared. He didn't have time to stop before he too had blundered over the edge of a deep hole.

He landed in a river of molten rock – there's a lot of that towards the centre of the Earth. But trolls are almost indestructible, so to Ogbuff it was like floating in warm treacle. The swift current carried the cook on. Bobbing ahead were Prince Tyran and the sergeant, travelling across underground plains of boiling mud and steam. It was pleasantly warm.

This must be where we trolls originally came from, Prince Tyran thought. It's nice. Great pools of sizzling metal roared and gushed around him as he drifted peacefully.

After a while the trolls heard a distant squeaking noise. They looked up – and this is what they saw.

They were really floating about on the inside of a large circular cave – it was as though the centre of the Earth was a great round room, and they were on one of the walls.

In the middle of the round space, a large creature was turning a handle. There were a lot of cogwheels round the handle, and a long thick axle that disappeared into the floor. The axle turned slowly on a large ball bearing, but the ball bearing was the Fire Opal, now glowing with a bright blue light.

'Is this yours?' said the creature who was turning the handle. He peered at them through the mist.

'Er – yes, sir,' said Tyran.

'You're trolls, aren't you? It was trolls who took the bearing away – centuries ago, you know. They came right down here, took one look at the ball bearing and picked it up.' He pointed at the Fire Opal, now blushing all the colours of the rainbow. 'It's very difficult, you know, keeping the world turning without it. It squeaks and shakes, and needs oil.'

'How long have you been turning that handle?' asked the sergeant breathlessly.

'It's a family tradition. I'm Gravendersop the 1045th.'

'The Fire Opal has been the Crown Jewel in our crown for centuries,' said Tyran. 'We'd be lost without it.'

'We followed it all day from our mountain,' said Ogbuff.

'At great expense to our feet,' added the sergeant.

'Well, perhaps we can come to some agreement,' said Gravendersop the 1045th.

'For the Opal we'll give you – um – a ton of gold,' said the prince.

Gravendersop the 1045th went on operating the world-turning handle with one hand and rubbed his nose with the other. 'There's lots of gold here at the centre of the Earth,' he said at last. 'Only it's better when you get near the surface. It's brighter.'

'How about diamonds and emeralds?' asked the sergeant.

'No thank you. They grow like weeds down here.'

The trolls huddled together and whispered among themselves.

'Well, what do you want for the Opal?' said Tyran at last.

'I've been turning the world round ever since my father – Gravendersop the 1044th – passed away,' said Gravendersop. 'I'll give you the Opal if you'll do my turning for me for five minutes while I take a break, then find a suitable rock to take its place.'

The trolls agreed, and climbed up the machinery to the handle. It took the three of them to turn it, while Gravendersop sat down beside them and lit his pipe.

'Phew, this is hard work,' gasped Ogbuff.

'Don't slow down,' said Gravendersop. 'If you do the world will stop, there'll be earthquakes and floods, and everyone will be flung off into outer space.'

'The five minutes are nearly up,' panted Tyran Ogg.

'Well now,' said Gravendersop, 'I don't think I want to start turning the world again *or* go and hunt for another stone. I think I'll have a little holiday . . .'

'Here, come back—' began the trolls, as he started to walk away. Gravendersop had cheated them!

For a moment they let go of the handle—

And the world stopped.

There was a click from the machinery, the Fire Opal bounced out, and the trolls were whirled away on a great gust of wind. There was nothing they could do about it.

They heard Gravendersop yelling at them as they bounced past him, but they could not stop as they were hurled away through the tunnels. Faster and faster they went, spinning in the wind until they shot out of the ground like bullets.

In the distance they could see Whitehelm Mountain, but it was moving. Everything was spinning off the Earth now that it had stopped, and with a crash the mountain rose like a rocket. The trolls went too, up through the clouds and away from Earth.

It seemed to Tyran Ogg that he was roaring through space for days before he landed upside down in a heap of dust. He crawled out spluttering.

In front of him lay a wide valley of white ash, full of craters. In the distance he saw a line of jagged mountains and above them, hanging in a skyful of stars, was the Earth.

He was on the moon! His dream had finally come true.

A moment later the mountains landed with a thud, bouncing trolls all over the place, and the Fire Opal smashed into some rocks.

None of the trolls were hurt, of course, because
they are almost indestructible. There's no water
or air on the moon, but that didn't bother them,
because they only breathed when they felt like it.
The first thing they did was put the Fire Opal back
in Tyran Ogg's crown and proclaim him King of the
Moon which, because it was so rocky, was a real
paradise for them.

They never found out what happened to

Gravendersop the 1045th, but since the world is going round he must still be turning the handle.

Or maybe now it is Gravendersop the 1046th . . . ?

LORD CAKE AND THE BATTLE FOR BANWEN'S BEACON

You've all heard of Llandanffwnfafegettupagogo, the little border town in the Wild West of England, and how it became famous in the Great Coal Rush of 1881 . . .

It became a boom town, with wild gambling parties and drinking in the rip-roaring Temperance Hotel, often until as late as 9 p.m. There were sheep rodeos too, and every day wagon trains left to cross the wild wet mountains and colonize the fertile valleys of Aberystwyth and Fishguard.

But the full story of the Coal Rush has never been told. Well, it will be now.

It was a wild grey Welsh day when the peace of the old public bar was disturbed by wild cries of:

'Coal! Coal! It's coal, look you, isn't it.'

Everyone rushed to the window. Down the street galloped a big shaggy carthorse, and on its back was a little man covered in coal dust from head to foot. In one hand he waved a great big nugget of coal.

By the time he reached the Assay Office half the town was following him. An assay office, as you probably know, is where gold prospectors can find out if the gold they find really is gold, and how much it is worth. Only this one was for coal, of course.

'Pure anthracite!' said the man at the office. 'Worth as much as two pounds a ton* – where did you find it?'

'Up on Banwen's Beacon,' said the little prospector. 'I'd just like to stake my claim, please. My name's Rupert Pullover.'

Anthracite! The news whizzed around the town like a bullet, and soon everyone was loading up their donkeys with picks and shovels and claim jumpers.†

---

* This was a *lot* of money. A typical labourer might only earn £30 in a whole *year*.

† A claim jumper is what miners used to wear to keep them warm.

Banwen's Beacon was a large bald hill above the village. A wide seam of coal came almost to the surface there, and all Rupert Pullover had done was dig down through the turf.

It wasn't long before all work had stopped in the village. The clang of picks and shovels floated down from the beacon and every sheep and cart for miles around was hauled in to take the coal away.

Everything would have been fine if a tall man wearing a forbidding bowler hat hadn't climbed up the hill. He called out to all the miners to stop work.

'As Clerk of the County Council,' he said, 'I have to tell you all that you are trespassing.'

'But this is common land,' said Rupert Pullover. 'It doesn't belong to anyone!'

'According to papers deposited at our offices this morning,' said the clerk, 'it belongs to Lord Cake. I should clear off if you don't want to be up

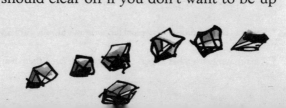

before the magistrates tomorrow.'

Lord Cake owned a big sheep farm not far from Llandanffwnfafegettupagogo and was a well-known local cheat and general nuisance.

'How can it belong to Lord Cake?' asked Dai Taten,* the village grocer, now also a prospector with everyone else in the village. 'It's not belonged to anyone for hundreds of years, boyo.'

'It's all legal,' said the clerk, and hurried off before they started to throw things.

'Let's get back down to the village and see about this!' said Dai.

Rupert Pullover, Dai Taten and the other prospectors rushed down to the village.

'It's true,' said the man in the Assay Office. 'Just after you came in shouting about finding coal one of Lord Cake's men brought in the deeds of the Beacon hills. That means he owns Banwen's

* Tommy Taten's great-grandfather, as it happens.

Beacon, and if you dig up that coal you might be put in prison.'

'But Banwen's Beacon doesn't belong to anyone, boyo,' said Dai Taten.

'The papers said it belonged to Lord Cake.'

'It's a rotten fiddle,' said Rupert Pullover, when they were outside again.

Just then the door of the saloon bar swung open, and out came Lord Cake with his bailiffs behind him. He resembled a large pudding and had a face as red as a cherry. When he walked, he wobbled so much that he looked like he would fall over.

'I heard you, Pullover,' he growled. 'It's about time you little coalminers were taught a lesson. I'm going to have the Great Western Railway brought through the village to take the coal away, and you can't stop me. Hahahahaha.'*

'You know Banwen's Beacon doesn't really

---

* Lord Cake had a particularly nasty laugh, the sort that makes your teeth tingle.

belong to you,' said Rupert.

'I'll tell you what,' said Lord Cake. 'If you can prove Banwen's Beacon doesn't belong to me, then you'll be able to mine coal there, won't you?'

And with another evil laugh he waddled away down the High Street.

'There's an old map in the bank,' whispered Dai, 'that'll show who Banwen's Beacon belongs to!'

But when they got to the bank, there was Lord Cake!

'Well, well,' he said. 'If you're looking for a certain map, well, it's locked in the vaults, and since I've just bought the bank . . .' He grinned nastily.

That night the miners held a meeting in the public bar. It was a typical Wild West saloon, with people gambling huge sums at dominoes and darts, and someone playing cheerful tunes on the piano.*

* 'She'll Be Coming Through the Sheepdip When She Comes' was a particular favourite.

'So it's all agreed,' said Rupert. 'To get the map, tomorrow morning we rob the bank.'

'Can't we pinch a bit of money too?' asked Dai.

'Just the map.'

'Waste of an opportunity, if you ask me,' said Dai.

'Now, you all know what you've got to do?' asked Rupert. 'One-arm Evans and Black-eye Morgan'll attract the attention of Police Constable Hodgkins while me and Dai rob the bank, and Tom'll have our getaway bicycles waiting outside.' He looked around at them all, then added, 'We've only got one chance, so things had better go well! Otherwise Lord Cake will have our coal.'

Tomorrow came, and Rupert Pullover's plan for stealing the map from Llandanffwnfafegettupagogo bank went into action.

Rupert and Dai Taten waited outside the bank until it opened. Then, with spotted handkerchiefs over their faces and brandishing pistols bought only that morning from the toy shop, they rushed in.

'Reach for the sky, pardner,'

said Dai, waving his pistol at the manager.

'Eh?'

Rupert Pullover felt a bit of a fool. 'Stop putting your hands in the air and open the safe,' he said. 'We don't want your money, just the map.'

'Lord Cake said I wasn't to let it out of my sight,' said the manager.

'We'll fill you full of holes, boyo,' said Dai, who was really enjoying himself.

But Rupert took the manager's keys and started to open the safe. Now the news of the robbery was spreading like an out-of-control fire, and when PC

Hodgkins at the police station heard it he rushed out on his bike.

Only to find that someone had let his tyres down. It was all part of the plan.

He puffed up to the bank just as Rupert and Dai were escaping on their getaway bicycles.

But Lord Cake had heard the commotion too, and he knew it could mean only one thing. Sooner than it takes to tell, he and his men were cycling madly in pursuit of our heroes.

'We'll take a short cut and head them off at the library!' he bawled.

Faster went Rupert and Dai, but Cake and his cronies were gaining on them.

Up Banwen's Beacon they went, and whizzed back up the High Street to the Assay Office.

'Here is the map,' panted Rupert, throwing it over the counter. 'It proves that Banwen's Beacon doesn't belong to anyone.'

'It belongs to the whole village,' puffed Dai.

Lord Cake came wobbling in, very out of breath, but a crowd of miners rushed up and caught him by his coat. Up came PC Hodgkins too.

'You haven't robbed any banks today, by any chance?' he said, looking closely at Rupert.

'Absolutely not. Really. A masked man dropped this from his bicycle,' said Rupert, who had stuffed his mask into his pocket. 'But arrest that man for forgery and claim jumping. *And* riding a bike without a bell, now I come to think of it.'

So all the miners were able to go up on Banwen's Beacon and each was able to mine his own mine.

And that was how the Great Coal Rush started.

THE TIME-TRAVELLING TELEVISION

Odd things happened in Blackbury. Things like this . . .

One bright Friday morning only a few years ago a man in a bright yellow jacket and safety helmet came to see Professor Miriam Oxford, curator of the Blackbury Museum.

'Good morning,' he said, 'I'm Fred Robertson,

and I'm the foreman up at the Sand and Gravel Quarry on Even Moor. We thought you'd like to see this.'

He opened the bag he was carrying and plonked a huge great fossil shell on the professor's desk. (The fossil was one of those curly ones, like a snail shell.)

'What a fine specimen!' said Professor Oxford.

'Yes, but you listen to it,' said Fred.

'Listen to it? Oh, you mean like we used to do with the seashells when we were kids? Well, that's a lot of nonsense, really.'

But Professor Oxford listened. Now, if you put a seashell to your ear you hear the sound of the sea. You know that. So if it's a fossilized seashell you can hear the sound of the sea as it was millions of years ago, when the waves broke on strange and curious seashores. And the professor heard the ancient

sea, and the puffing and grunting of reptiles on the shore, and the cries of things which surely couldn't have been seagulls.

'You listen on,' said Fred. 'You ain't heard nothing yet.'

With her mouth open the professor went on listening. And above the pounding of the surf she heard a voice, singing 'Has Anybody Here Seen Kelly?'*

She began to sing along with the voice:

'He's as bad as old Antonio,
Left me on my own-ee-o,
Has anybody here seen Kelly?
Kelly from the Isle—'

She stopped, remembering how she couldn't really sing very well.† **'Incredible!'** she said.

'That's what we all thought,' said Fred. 'Sometimes he sings, and sometimes he whistles.

---

* An old music-hall song about a woman from the Isle of Man looking for her boyfriend.

† Very true. She couldn't carry a tune in a bucket.

That's not all we found. Look here.'
He produced a pair of fossilized sun-
glasses, and a fossilized copy of the

BLACKBURY AND WEST GRITSHIRE GAZETTE,

dated next Monday. The paper was hard as a
lump of slate, but you could still just make
out the writing.

'They were with the shell,' said Fred.

'Well, I've never—' began the professor.

There was suddenly a terrific commotion in the
street outside. There was a prehistoric monster
walking down the High Street! It was slightly
transparent – walking through things without
harming them – but of course, that's no great consol-
ation. It was only there for a few minutes before it
went **fuzzy** and vanished.

'Hmm, a triceratops,' said the professor. 'A

harmless herbivore – it eats veg, I mean. What's going on?'

After that first day some very odd things started to happen around Blackbury. There was the static electricity, for one thing. It didn't hurt anybody, but everything in the town sometimes hummed and crackled as though it was in a thunderstorm. And several times ghostly prehistoric monsters wandered through the town as if it wasn't there, like great big ghosts.

And sometimes from the fossilized seashell on Professor Oxford's desk would come the voice of someone singing 'Has Anybody Here Seen Kelly?'

on an ancient and far-off seashore.

The professor called a special meeting.

'There's no doubt about it,' she said. 'The fossilized newspaper we found proved it. Someone has gone back in time millions of years, probably to where the Sand and Gravel Quarry is now. You've found some other fossils, haven't you?'

'Yes,' said Fred Robertson, the site foreman. 'Yesterday we found a fossilized deckchair. This bloke must have left it there. But the oddest thing is up at the site. You'd better come and look.'

They went up to the quarry on the mysterious Even Moor – and there they saw the seashore.

Millions of years before there had been a muddy sea over most of what was now South Gritshire,

and the shore had come up to Even Moor. Then it had hardened into stone. It was quite usual for quarry workers to find dinosaur footprints in it. But what Fred pointed out was the fossilized footprint of a left-hand wellington boot.

'That settles it,' said Miriam Oxford. 'Someone from our time has discovered some kind of time-travel. Just think of the possibilities for science! We've got to find them!' She stared around. There was only one house near the quarry.

'That belongs to old Bill Posters,' said Fred. 'He's an old-age pensioner. I shouldn't think he knows anything about this. He collects butterflies, you know.'

'Hush!' hissed the professor.

From the cottage suddenly came the sound of someone whistling a familiar tune – 'Has Anybody Here Seen Kelly?'

'It's him!' shouted the professor, dashing towards the cottage and banging on the door. Immediately her hair stood on end and blue sparks flashed from her fingers.

Then she realized that the door wasn't really locked. Inside, the cottage was dark and rather dusty and full of ornaments. An old-fashioned television was on in the corner, but its screen was all crackly and fuzzy, as though it wasn't tuned in properly. There were the remains of someone's breakfast – a boiled egg – on the table, and a white cat was dozing in front of the fire.

Professor Oxford stormed around the house. There was no one there. Then she heard the singing again. It seemed to be coming from outside the back door this time, so she wrenched it open – and stepped out into blazing sunlight.

She was standing on a beach of orange sand.

A sluggish, muddy sea broke on the shore, and in the yellow sky the sun looked white and bigger than usual. There were grey cliffs in the distance and, not far from the shore, something big and finny was wallowing in the sea.

The professor still had her hand on the door handle. She hurriedly stepped back, slammed the door behind her and then leaned against it.

'Now, I must think slowly about this,' she said to herself. 'Here is a kitchen. It's musty and rather dark, and this is the twenty-first century, and this is twenty-one miles from the sea.'

She opened the door a crack. Where the grey fields of Even Moor should have been the sea was still rolling in.

'But that looks very much like millions of years ago,' she said in wonder.

'I say! Hello there!' shouted a man who was paddling in the sea. He had his trousers rolled up to his knees, a handkerchief knotted on his head and a butterfly net in his hand.

Professor Oxford stepped through the door again, and onto the sand. The man with the butterfly net came trotting towards her and shook her hand.

'Well well well,' he said. 'Do you know, you're the first person I've seen for days!'

'You must be Bill Posters,' said the professor.

'That's me!' said Bill Posters. 'I say, there's some

yellow butterflies over here with wings almost a metre across – very odd.'

As they walked across the sand, the professor gazed intently at lizards and shells, and at last she said: 'This proves it. Your back door somehow opens onto a beach several hundred million years ago! I doubt if there are even any dinosaurs yet.'

'Amazing,' said Bill Posters. 'You know, I've wondered a bit myself. I thought at first this was some kind of South Sea island.'

A giant blue and green dragonfly swooped overhead.

'It's my old television that caused this, I think,' said Bill. 'Did you see it on when you went indoors? There was a sizzling noise in it the other week and now every time you switch it on you get all this' – he waved an arm at the sea, sand and yellow sky – 'just outside the back door.'

A small blue beetle trotted over the sand. The sun was very hot.

'Of course, if anyone was to switch it off while we were here we could be stuck,' said Bill Posters conversationally.

They glanced back at the hazy outline of the cottage on the beach. And inside, as the worried men from the quarry came in to look for the professor, one of them turned the fuzzy television off. The cottage disappeared.

'Oh dear,' said Bill Posters.

Well, at first it wasn't too bad. They made a fire out of dried seaweed and ferns, and scraped giant limpets off the rocks to make a fish stew which was really rather good. The sun set and the stars came out – and they were a lot brighter and quite different from the ones we get today. Bill sang his

favourite song again, and they fell into a peaceful sleep.

Next morning they thought they had better explore in case there were any dangerous animals around. The great young sun blazed down as they strolled along the beach, and odd winged lizards whizzed overhead. Everything was very fresh and new. Out in the sea curious sea creatures snorted and splashed.

'This would be just the place to retire to,' said Bill Posters.

The professor grunted. She was really more interested in filling her pockets with shells and stones and bits of grass and thinking of the enormously interesting scientific things she'd be able to do if ever she got back to Blackbury University.

Around lunch time they clambered over some rocks at the end of the bay and Bill Posters wiped his brow and said, 'I'd really like a glass of lemonade about now.'

And in front of them they saw, up against a grey cliff, a pub. It was thatched. Roses grew around the door. There was a painted sign in front of it which said THE DOG AND DINOSAUR.

'It's the sun,' said Professor Oxford. 'It's affecting our heads. That is a figment of our imagination.'

'Well, I'm going to have a figment of iced lemonade,' said Bill, and set off at a trot.

Inside the Dog and Dinosaur it was cool and dim, and a little man in a white coat was polishing glasses behind the bar.

'Good morning,' he said conversationally. 'Another lovely day. Of course, it always is here. When are you from?'

The professor and Bill Posters looked out at the grey sea and the big young sun.

'Er . . . what do you mean, *when* are we from?' asked the professor after a pause.

The barman of the Dog and Dinosaur said, 'Don't you know? How did you get here? Wonky television method, I suppose. Oh. Here, you're not Bill Posters, are you?'

Bill said 'Yes' because things had got beyond him.

The barman grinned, and shook their hands. Then he explained how Bill's discovery that a wonky television could produce time-travelling had become world famous. And once the doors to time-travel were opened, why, *everyone* wanted to have a go too.

He himself was from 2055, said the barman, and by his time millions of people were time-travelling. That was why he had opened his pub in the Carbonaceous Age.

'Most people spend their holidays in the Jurassic Period,' he added. 'The dinosaurs, you know. Interesting. Very popular.* We really get more senior citizens here, like your good old selves. It's so peaceful. Nothing much is due to happen on this stretch of seashore for another million years.'

'I say, can you get us back home?' asked the professor.

'Of course,' said the barman. 'But come back soon. Bring some friends!' He twiddled a dial on

---

* Though also sometimes fatal, since time-travel doesn't necessarily mean travel without risks, and a hungry T. Rex often likes nothing better than to snack on an unwary tourist.

a shelf, there was a slight *zipppp!* and the familiar outline of Even Moor, all grey and heathery, appeared in a doorway.

A moment after they stepped through they were alone. And then they were back in Bill's kitchen.

Well, everything that happened next had to happen. Soon a party of scientists from Blackbury University were studying Bill's wonky television to find out how the time-travelling worked. Miriam Oxford spent a lot of time on news programmes too, explaining it all.

And Bill Posters?

He disappeared mysteriously, leaving a little note that only the professor understood. It said:

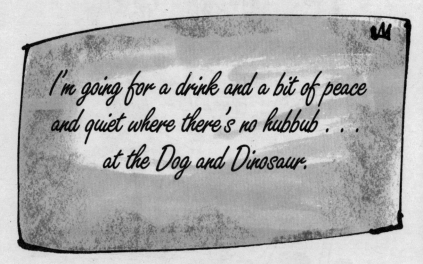

I'm going for a drink and a bit of peace and quiet where there's no hubbub . . . at the Dog and Dinosaur.

THE BLACKBURY PARK STATUES

Back in the day, Blackbury Park (NO SINGING, DANCING OR RIDING, BY ORDER) was closed every night at six o'clock with a big green padlock.

It was dark and lonely inside. Shadows lurked among the rhododendron bushes, played across the silent waters of the boating lake and hung between the flower beds.

'Go on, push off, you great booby!'

The voice came from a statue on a pedestal, in a clump of rhododendrons by the lake. A bronze plaque said it was of Lord Palmerston. The statue – a Victorian-looking man in early trousers and frock coat – was flailing wildly at a pigeon with a marble scroll.

'Go away! Get off! You ought to be in a pie!'

The statue jumped down from his pedestal and clumped heavily to the pool edge, where he removed his boots and cooled his feet in the dark water, with a sigh of relief.

All over the park the other statues were waking up. There was a neigh as General Sir George Balaclava, horse and all, leaped down from his plinth and cantered across the lawns. Sir Harold Pincer, cast in bronze, strolled pompously past.

A couple of marble water nymphs picked flowers; a lion, carved in millstone grit, stood up and shook his mane.

Soon the park was alive with movement, the air filled with talking and laughter. In the middle of it all sat Lord Palmerston, soaking his feet.

'She wasn't there again today, Leo,' he said, as the lion padded up. 'I'm getting worried. It's been nearly a week now.'

'That's odd. She even comes here at Christmas time,' growled the lion.

'Who's this?' asked a bronze nymph, who lived at the other side of the park.

'Mrs Mince,' said Lord Palmerston. 'The old lady who comes in to feed the ducks of a morning. She's been coming to the park ever since I remember – even when she was a little girl. There were only a few of us here in those days,' he added wistfully.

'She used to come courting here with that young man what got killed in the war – the first one,' said the lion.

'Then she married that fellow from East Slate,' said Lord Palmerston.

By now quite a crowd had gathered.

'She used to bring her kids in to play,' said General Sir George Balaclava, whose plinth over-looked the children's playground.

'And her grandchildren,' said Sir Harold Pincer.

'She must be very, very old now,' said Lord Palmerston, drying his feet on the lion's mane. 'I hope nothing's happened to her.'

'Does anyone know where she lives?' asked Sir George.

'Number seven, Mafeking Terrace,' said the lion. 'I heard her talking about it to someone once.'

'Are you suggesting that we go and look?' asked

Lord Palmerston. 'That's risky. Still . . . she has been here thousands of times. Let's wait until tomorrow. She might come back.'

All the next day the statues in Blackbury Park waited for Mrs Mince. They stood as still as – well, statues – watching the visitors, but there was no sign of the old lady.

As soon as the gate was locked for the night Lord Palmerston jumped down from his pedestal.

'Right,' he said, 'who's going to come with me to Mafeking Terrace?'

'It ought to be me,' said bronze Sir George Balaclava. 'I've got a horse.'

'Then take me too,' said Lord Palmerston, and a couple of water nymphs helped him onto the metal horse. 'How are we going to get out?' he asked as they **cantered off**.

For an answer, Sir George spurred his horse and next moment it was thundering towards the fence.

It landed on the other side in a shower of sparks. **'Wheee!'** said Sir George. 'I haven't enjoyed anything so much since the Battle of Balaclava – where I was shot dead, as I seem to remember.'

There was no traffic, which was a good thing since they were riding down the middle of the road.

'Here, you don't think she's dead?' said Lord Palmerston after a while.

'That would be all right – they'll make a statue of her then.'

'You've got to be famous or decorative for that, and I don't think she was really either.'

Sir George reined his horse in by a policeman. 'We're looking for Mafeking Terrace, Officer,' he said. 'Could you direct us?'

'Just down the street and second on the left,' said the policeman. 'That's a fine horse.'

'Tends to squeak,' said Sir George, as they rode away.

They soon found Mafeking Terrace, and Lord Palmerston hammered on the door of number seven. Since he was seven feet high and made of marble this made rather a din, but no one answered.

The window of number nine shot up.

'If you're looking for Mrs Mince, she passed away on Saturday,' said the neighbour. "Ere, who are you anyway?'

But Sir George and Lord Palmerston were already galloping away through the dark streets of Blackbury.

Eventually they reached Blackbury cemetery, and leaped over the gates.

'He's always here,' said Lord Palmerston, looking

about. 'Haven't visited him in years, but he— Ah, there he is.'

'He' was carved from white marble, and was an angel in the family vault of the Lords of Gritshire. Most of the statues in there were of angels or cherubs, which rather embarrassed Lord Palmerston, used as he was to the hurly-burly of the park.*

'Good evening, Pietro,' he said to the angel he was looking for. He removed his hat.

The angel nodded, and smiled. 'It's a long time since we've seen you in here,' he said, removing nothing since he was wearing nothing.

'Er – yes, well, it's been a busy time at the park,' said Lord Palmerston. 'Er – have you had a Mrs Mince brought in?'

'Yes, plot thirty-two in row forty,' said the angel. 'Dear old soul.'

---

* And to the fact that almost everyone in the park was fully dressed, while the angels were lacking any clothes. And Lord Palmerston was a very proper gentleman who did not think it right to see an unclothed body.

the Lords of Gnthire

'We were a bit worried because she stopped coming to the park,' said Sir George. 'I suppose there is no way of getting a statue made? I mean, I was human once, and now I'm a statue. I'm sure she'd enjoy being in the park. She used to spend nearly all her time there anyway.'

The angel sat down and folded his wings. 'I don't expect she did anything to get people to make a statue of her, like shooting guns and going on and on in Parliament.' He smiled. 'You know her – can you think of anything?'

'Only something like FOR SERVICES TO FEEDING DUCKS,' said Sir George.

'Just a moment, though,' said Lord Palmerston. 'When she was young she used to chain herself to railings for votes for women. She was a big leader of the Suffragettes* of Blackbury. Chained herself to the park railings twice, and to the park keeper

*The Suffragettes were an inspirational group who successfully campaigned for women's rights to vote.

once. Threw mud at Prime Minister Asquith. Oh, she really fought for the vote. I'm just glad I wasn't Prime Minister at the time.'

'Well, people have had statues made for much less,' said the angel.

'Trouble is, what can we do? We don't look human enough to go and see the Town Clerk,' said Lord Palmerston.

'Use the public phone box by the park gates. I'll tell you how to use it,' said the angel. 'You'll need to put money in to use it – sixpence,* I think – and you have to reach him during the day. You might find some coins in the park, if you look where people have dropped them. Try the wishing pool.'

Sir George and Lord Palmerston looked at each other.

'It's worth a try,' said Lord Palmerston.

---

* A sixpence – often called a tanner – was an old coin used when British money was divided into pounds, shillings and pence and you really did have to know your twelve times table to work out how much things cost. I used this coinage when I was a young boy, and I still sometimes long for the days when I could jingle a couple of tanners in my pocket along with a chunky thrupenny bit or two. Today's pound coins don't jangle in the same way.

*

Lord Palmerston had trouble using the telephone box. Since he was seven foot high and carved out of marble he found it difficult to dial, for one thing. His fingers were too big.

The statues had had a **big** meeting in the park the previous night, and decided that Lord Palmerston shouldn't phone the Town Clerk but something called the British Political History Society. A statue of William Makeworthy, the twentieth Mayor of Blackbury, said that the Society were just the type to go around erecting statues.

'I've only got one sixpence,' said Lord Palmerston. 'And that's worn **thin**.'

Anyway, he finally got through to the Society.

'This is Lord— This is Mr John Smith speaking, I mean,' he said. 'I think you should know that Mrs

Mince has died. You know, she did a lot for votes for women.'

'Mrs Mince?' said the secretary. 'Of course. Dear me.'

'We thought a statue in the park would be appropriate,' said Lord Palmerston. 'She often used to visit there, you know.'

'Actually, we were thinking of this ourselves,' said the secretary. 'What did you say your name was, sir?'

But Lord Palmerston had put the receiver down and was hurrying back to the park, greatly surprising a young lady who was waiting to use the phone box.

The others were waiting for him. Since it was daylight they were all standing still on their pedestals, but they moved their eyes as he rushed past waving his hands in the victory salute. Then he leaped onto his plinth while the park keeper's back was turned, picked up the marble scroll he had been holding, and in a moment was looking as though he hadn't moved in a hundred years.

They waited all that summer, and through to the following spring. It was late in February, when Lord Palmerston was dozing under a light coating of snow, that the packing case arrived. A new pedestal was set up down by the ornamental fountain and something shrouded in a cloth was cemented to it.

The Mayor and the President of the British Political History Society turned up, with photographers and a crowd of people. There were several speeches . . . and then the Mayor unveiled Mrs Mince.

The statues gasped, and the crowd clapped politely.

'Of course!' said Lord Palmerston to himself. 'The sculptor's shown her as she was when she was a Suffragette!'

The statue was of a much younger Mrs Mince in an Edwardian dress and a gigantic hat, chained to a piece of railing and wearing a defiant expression.

When everyone else had gone home the statues rushed to greet her.

Lord Palmerston broke the handcuffs and helped her down.

'Here, I recognize you!' the Suffragette said in

delight. 'All of you. Isn't this the park?'

'Dear Mrs Mince, let me explain,' said Lord Palmerston.

And he did. Then, as the moon came up, the statue of Pan and the statue of Menuenchi the violinist* turned up and started to play a waltz, Lord Palmerston swept up Mrs Mince in his arms and they swirled out among the dancing statues over the park keeper's carefully mown, snow-dusted grass.

* Often confused with the violinist Yehudi Menuhin, Menuenchi was nowhere near as famous, but had been a very fine fiddler indeed for the Blackbury Pit Band.

WIZARD WAR

Jack was walking through the wood when a spell passed him, heading south.

Now it's easy to see spells, if you've been trained to do so, and since Jack was a wizard's apprentice he knew a spell when he saw it. This one looked like – well, if I say it looked like a small red cloud of fog, full of little twinkling lights, that's about as close as you'll get.

Oh dear, it's Mallebor sending spells again, thought Jack, and he hurried after the spell.

He followed it through the wood and up the hill. On top of the hill was a stone tower, and just as Jack reached its big oak door the spell popped in through the window. There was a *pop!* from inside, a heavy thud, and someone started to swear in a loud voice.

'Newt's teeth! I'll give him collapsing magic—!'

Jack pushed open the door. There, on the floor, was a chair. But all its legs were broken. And sitting on the floor was a furious wizard.

His name was Robellam, and his face was red with anger. In fact his anger had turned white with rage, and then his rage turned purple with fury, because he realized that his arch-enemy Mallebor had struck again.

To understand the great war between the two wizards it's necessary to know about wizards in general. Wizards are very proud. The better they are the prouder they become, until they can't stand other wizards.

Well, Robellam lived in a tower above the little village of Chepping Outfeathers, and everything had been peaceful until Mallebor moved into another tower across the valley (wizards always live in towers).

From then on there had been nothing but trouble. Sometimes it was just a Grade Four spell, to sour the milk or turn the other wizard's nose green, but when one of them became really angry . . .

'Jack!'

bawled Robellam. 'Bring me my wand, my book and my cauldron! I'll show him who he's dealing with! A Grade *Three* spell, I think.'

Oh dear, thought Jack again.

Soon he had to open a window to let the Grade Three spell out. It hovered just outside, a blue ball

flashing with green lights.

'Go and turn his front door to cheese!' **thundered** Robellam.

'He'll only send back a Grade *Two*, sir. He always does,' said Jack. 'And you know what a Grade Two does. It turns—'

'Go down to the village again and buy a dozen eggs, boy,' said the wizard coldly. 'I'm quite capable of dealing with any spells that ridiculous charlatan can make, thank you.'

Jack was glad to get out of the tower. It was always best to leave the two wizards alone until they got fed up. Usually they resorted to threatening letters after the first exchange of Grade Two spells.

As he entered the grocer's he met a ginger cat with a particularly fine tail. It was Geryboam, Mallebor's assistant.

'G'morning, Jack. I see they're at it again,' said the cat.

'Second time this week,' agreed Jack. 'We ought to do something about it. It's ruining my education.'

'What can we do?' asked Geryboam. 'I can only make a Grade Five spell, and only on certain days of the week at that. What do you suggest?'

'We can't stop them fighting,' said Jack. 'No one – well, except for the Great Wizard himself, of course – can make a wizard do anything he doesn't want to do. I've got to buy a dozen eggs, and I know that's part of the recipe for a Roof and Ceiling Enchantment, so you'd better hide in the coalhouse.'

'Well, I've got to buy a bag of pepper,' said Geryboam, 'and that's part of my master's Floors and Doors Spell, so you'd better hide in the attic.'

There was a crackling sound, and a ball of green fire zipped overhead in the direction of Robellam's tower. A second later a small flock of golden stars passed the other way, heading for Mallebor. At the same time the window of the grocer's shop turned to pink ice, and began to melt.

'Oh dear, side effects,' said Geryboam.

'I think we owe it to the community to put a stop to this,' said Jack importantly. He concentrated on the window, and with a great effort turned it back to glass again before the grocer noticed.

When Jack got back to Robellam's tower it was in a terrible state. Several badly aimed spells had landed in the garden, and inside the tower not one stick of furniture was in one piece. The carpets had rolled themselves up, and there was a smell of burning boots, broomsticks, bookshelves and beams. Robellam was striding up and down muttering to himself. He snatched the eggs from Jack and disappeared into his study.

Then Jack threw all his possessions into a bag and hurried back out, slamming the door behind him just as it turned to treacle.

He met Geryboam, as they had agreed, in the wood. The cat had a small bag of fish heads tied to his collar.

'You realize, of course, that an apprentice who leaves his wizard without notice is subject to Being Turned into a Beetle under the Wizards and Warlocks Act of 1872?' asked Geryboam, with a wave of his tail.

'I'm trying to do a Grade Four spell,' said Jack. 'Be quiet for a minute.'

'I just want you to know that if your plan doesn't work I want no part of it—'

Suddenly there was a *flash!* and a **bang!** The next moment they

were standing on a bleak mountain. Strange stars of unheard-of colours shone overhead, and on top of the mountain was the house of the Great Wizard. They were in the Land of Lume, the magic place that is as far and near our time as the other side of a shadow.

'You've done it now,' hissed Geryboam.

'No one can make a wizard do anything he doesn't want to do, except the Great Wizard,' said Jack. 'We *have* to see him.'

He hurried up the path towards the bleak house, and presently Geryboam followed him. There didn't seem to be any choice.

They came to the door of the Great Wizard's house. It was made of iron, and studded with uncut diamonds. There was a brass door knocker in the shape of a lion's head, and when Jack used it the door shook with a noise like thunder.

The brass lion said, 'Well, what do you want?'

'The door knocker spoke!' whispered Geryboam.

'We want the Great Wizard to help us end the battle between Robellam and Mallebor,' said Jack. 'If he doesn't mind, that is.'

The lion said nothing, but the door swung open, and the two apprentices found themselves in a large hallway. A grandfather clock ticked slowly in one corner, and there were wands and broomsticks in an umbrella stand.

It was very dark. Finally the grandfather clock said, 'Don't just stand there.'

Jack jumped. 'S-sorry,' he gasped.

'I should think so,' said the clock. 'Now then, these wizards – we agree they should be stopped. It's bad for trade. On the hall table you will find a bag containing two Grade One spells. That should put a stop to all this.'

'Wh-where's the Great Wizard?' asked Geryboam.

'Oh, he doesn't bother himself with spells.

He lets us furniture deal with them. I hope you know how to deal with spells,' the clock added. 'Of course, you yourself can't make spells any greater than Grade Four ones, I know, but you can use these as a special gift from the Great Wizard – one each, one for each wizard. We've been watching those two for some time, you know. In fact, Robellam's clock is a cousin of mine. They are very good spellmakers but that fighting gives the profession a bad name. Now then, step on the doormat.'

Jack picked up the bag of spells, stepped backwards, and *whump!* They were standing in the woods again. The Land of Lume had completely disappeared.

'Talking furniture!' said Geryboam. **'I'm glad our furniture knows its place!'**

'Two Grade One spells,' said Jack. 'They're very powerful! Even Robellam has to work hard to make one! I hope nothing happens to the wizards – old Robellam's quite a good master when he hasn't lost his temper.'

'So is Mallebor,' said Geryboam. 'When you think that a Grade One spell could turn him into a button, well, it's not right.'

'I don't think the Great Wizard will do that,' said Jack. 'Anyway, if they don't stop soon one of them will get hurt.'

'If you let those spells out of the bag we'll all be better off in Australia,' said Geryboam.

Jack and Geryboam crept quietly up the hill towards Robellam's tower, clutching the bag of spells. High above them something whizzed across the sky and knocked some tiles off the roof. It looked like a ball of red smoke.

'They're still at it,' said Geryboam. 'I must say,

my master Mallebor conjures up a good Bowers and Towers Spell.'

The garden was full of craters where spells had fallen. The lawn had turned an odd purply-green. The rockery had disappeared completely, leaving a blue haze, while the greenhouse – well, something very, very strange had happened to the greenhouse. And the crazy paving was definitely crazier than it had been before.

'Jack! Stop consorting with the enemy!' came a voice from the window, and they looked up to see Robellam in a tin helmet.

'Now?' said Jack.

'Why not?' said Geryboam, looking anxiously at the greenhouse.

Jack unfastened the string round the mouth of the bag and stood back.

For a moment nothing happened. Then the

sack bulged, and two small black globes floated up. They grew bigger and bigger, and it seemed to Jack that they weren't so much black as colourless – they seemed to suck in all the light around them. They hung above the tower, and then one of them drifted off across the valley, heading towards Mallebor's tower. The other sank through the roof of Robellam's tower.

'Oh, help,' croaked Jack. There was a howl, and Robellam whizzed through the door. He dodged the greenhouses, leaped the fence and disappeared down the valley with the spell after him, and Jack and Geryboam running after the spell.

They ran through the village street and there, coming the other way with his magic robes flying, was Mallebor. The two wizards met in the middle of the road, turned, and started casting spells at the black globes behind them. But the weaker spells just got sucked in.

The Grade One spells seemed to grow too, as they absorbed the magic.

Jack saw Mallebor turn to Robellam and say something, and then the wizards joined hands and started to spin round. Faster and faster they turned, until they were just a blur – and above them a white flame grew.

It spread until the air looked as though it was burning, and wrapped itself around the black spells. There was a *pop!* a sound like faraway thunder, and the two wizards sprawled in the dust.

'By Jove, that gave me a fright,' said Mallebor, dusting himself off and giving Robellam a helping hand. 'Thank goodness we could combine our forces to see them off. How are you?'

Robellam dusted off his robes. 'I am fine,

thank you,' he said. 'What has always puzzled me is what happens to the magic after the Flame of Cigam burns it,' he mused. 'I was surprised it worked just now – but I'd never have been able to do it without you.'

'Well now, I've got a few books which might be able to help,' said Mallebor. 'Shall we go and discuss this further?'

And they wandered off happily together.

'Cuppa tea?' said Jack, turning to the cat with a smile.

'I'll have a saucer of milk,' said Geryboam.

And they hurried after their masters.

THE EXTRAORDINARY
ADVENTURES
OF DOGGINS

Doggins lay on his stomach, sucking a straw and listening to the bees. It was summer time in the Dandoloone mountains, and a very peaceful day.

Suddenly he heard singing far off, and a sound like an angry wasp buzzing. Then he saw a curious zeppelin emerging from a small white cloud above the mountain. Doggins looked up at it in amazement. It was the first time he had seen anything like it.

It was shaped like a short, fat, straight banana, but painted in red and orange stripes, and with rigging like an ordinary ship. Underneath a gas bag hung a sort of wickerwork houseboat, with a propeller at the back and big bay windows in the front. At one of these someone was sitting on a platform outside and cleaning the glass industriously, while singing the first two lines of 'Rose of Dandoloone' over and over again because she didn't know the rest.*
Meanwhile the airship **glided** slowly to a halt about three metres above Doggins, and dropped anchor, which only just missed him.

The engine stopped. A hatch opened, and Doggins saw someone who appeared to be almost all beard and hat, wearing a captain's uniform.

'I say – excuse me a minute.'

* And neither do I, so I think we will have to leave it at that.

Doggins raised his own hat – he had been well brought up. 'Can I be of assistance?' he said.

'Thank you very much. Please tell me, where are we?' asked the captain.

'Well, these are the Dandoloone mountains, and this particular mountain you have landed on is called Tumbleover Hill. That's the Lurkledoom forest over there, and my name is Doggins – though I'm not really a kind of small dog, for it's an ancient and honourable name handed down by generations of noble Dogginses, and I live here except when I'm away from home, which is often, when I don't.' He went over the sentence again in his mind to see if it sounded right, decided it didn't, and added, 'If you catch my meaning.'

'Oh,' said the captain. 'Perhaps you could point it out on my map. Come aboard.'

He threw down a rope ladder and, after

deciding that it was safe, Doggins climbed up into the airship. It was quite big inside, with a stove and bunks, and a big gilt wheel for steering.

'Very nice thing you have here,' he said respectfully. 'What's it for?'

'It's my airship,' said the captain, 'for sailing in the air. I built it. We're on the way to the Hall-Doom Islands at the moment. Care to come? We could do with some more crew. Here today, then up and off again tomorrow. A sky ahead that is always changing.'

Doggins said he would think about it – it sounded like an **Awfully Big Adventure**. Then the captain showed him everything that he had invented, while Ella, the girl who had been cleaning the windows, came back in and went over to check some very complicated dials, twiddling a lever or two

to make some adjustments.

Outside the sun went down and the wind got up, and it seemed to Doggins that the airship was moving to and fro.

Well, he finally told the captain exactly where he had lost his way and got up to go. But when he opened the hatch, *he* was lost too. Where the grass of Tumbleover Hill should have been there was only black water, shining in the moonlight. The anchor rope had broken!

Doggins sat contentedly behind the captain as the airship chugged over the sea. It had been like that

for days. Sometimes they would go down a bit and open the hatch in the floor, so they could drop down the rope ladder and have a swim or go fishing. But mainly it was just sea, and sea, and more sea. 'Hallo,' said the captain suddenly. **'Look.'**

On the horizon was a dark smudge, with a snow-capped mountain in the middle of it. The captain spun the wheel so that the airship headed for it. The island was getting nearer and nearer and they could see a line of white breakers round the reef.

'Get the anchor ready,' the captain said.

'We lost it. Don't you remember?' said Ella.

'Hand me that shark-fishing line,' said Doggins, and he opened the hatch. He waited until a likely-looking tree came past, and dropped the end of the line into it. The fishing line was a thick one with

three hooks at the end, so it held them fast.

Cautiously they slid down the line. First came the captain, with a long knife clenched between his teeth (you never know, on unexplored islands), then Doggins, and finally Ella. They crept along in single file, listening. There was a cool breeze blowing through the woods, and a soft jingling noise started as the trees moved. And there were twinkles, and chimes, as if the whole wood was made of glass and silver. Soon, above the heads of our bold explorers, the trees were clanging and clanking away like a thousand church bells.

'I wonder— Ow!' said Doggins, and he rubbed his head.

'Sssh!' hissed the captain.

'I will not!' cried Doggins. 'Someone just threw something at me!' Something hit the ground by his foot, and bounced away. It was round and silver, and looked very much like a coin . . .

'A fifty-pence piece,' said the captain. 'That's ridiculous, because money does not grow on trees.'*

A particularly strong gust blew through the wood, and they were pelted with more falling coins.

'I'll believe it just this once,' said the captain, 'but I won't ever again.' He rubbed his ear where a ripe ten-p piece had caught it. But the thrill of

* As your parents might remind you on a regular basis.

'I've a strong suspicion that we're somewhere we shouldn't be,' said Doggins nervously. The three of them crept away into the bushes, and watched as the penny-pickers came into the glade.

Picking money looked quite easy. Men in green baize aprons put ladders up into some of the trees, and soon there was the sound of baskets being filled. All the time they sang their penny-picking song, while the jangling of the money in the breeze made a tinkling, thin sort of music.

'Want to have a look round?' said a voice behind them. Doggins turned round suddenly, and saw a small man in a white smock, holding a trowel in one hand and a seed basket in the other.

They said yes, and followed him out of the wood. He told them that he was one of the money cultivators, and they had landed in the middle of plucking time, when the ripe money was sent away to the Mint. As they walked between well-tended fields the captain and Ella wandered off to do some exploring on their own, after promising not to walk on any young plants.

Doggins was allowed into one of the large greenhouses that occupied the southern half of the island. There, more exotic specimens were grown. He watched fascinated as men watered the rare, beautiful fifty-pound notes, which had to be grown in special rich soil and pruned regularly, or else they just became the common five-pound notes. And there were clumps of real golden coins, and seed-boxes of silver shillings and Maundy money, and so on.

'If you let your money grow wild,' said the cultivator, whose name was Henry, 'you soon get square threepenny bits and suchlike. To say nothing of weeds – many of them being plants we used to value but no longer do. They don't like to die out, you know.' He pointed some out to Doggins. There was the hardy perennial farthing, and the old groat, and things that weren't even really weeds, but real plants in inconvenient places – like a Scottish ten-pound note and the creeping stinging, slinging old Australian penny (known scientifically as *Copperus Antipoedius*).

And so it went on for the rest of the day. The captain came in muddy and overjoyed because, after great digging and climbing, he had discovered a perfect specimen of *Fivus Bobbilius*, or an elusive, and very collectible, five-shilling piece. Henry very kindly let him keep it for his pressed plants collection, and he also gave Ella a sprig off a special sixpenny bush.

Then he looked hard at Doggins. 'The captain likes scientific things, and Ella likes small delicate things, but I don't know what you could find a use for,' he said. Finally he went off into a back room and returned holding a threepenny bit. 'This is a favourite old British piece of money,' he said, 'and what, I wonder, will you be able to grow with it?'*

Later, they climbed back up the rope ladder, cast off and floated away from the island.

'We never asked them where we were,' said the captain.

---

* Actually, Doggins planted it when he got back to the airship, and it grew into a small bush with white and purple flowers. It never grew any money, but it smelled nice.

'It doesn't matter,' said Doggins contentedly. 'Let's just go on and on.'

One evening in July, when the airship was floating over an uninteresting piece of land, a distant thunderclap made the captain drop what he was doing (he was trying to build an airship in a bottle).

He looked at the barometer: it was very low. Then he took out his watch with the luminous dial, and it was glowing brightly. There was a strong smell of electricity, and the captain could feel tiny shocks in the soles of his feet.

'We're in for a storm,' he said to himself. 'Ella – mizzen the starboard clothes line and hoist the umbrella stand. Doggins – belay the gas bag.'

Suddenly there was a rumbling, smashing, echoing, cracking, thundering, hanging, hammering, grinding, scraping, blood-curdling

CRASH!

'It's right above us!' shouted the captain. Blue sparks were flashing between Doggins' ears.

The electric storm raged around the airship, sometimes spinning it round and standing it on end. Doggins clung to the steering wheel and wished that he was somewhere else. A brilliant

flash of lightning zipped right by the gas bag, and the gold braid on the captain's uniform began to shine with an eerie green light.

'This is an emergency!' declared the captain, 'Doggins, pull the lever marked Up.'

He did, and for a moment nothing happened. Then every cylinder in the airship began to pump out gas at a furious rate. The ship shot up through the clouds like the fastest lift in the world, and the crew held on tightly as the air whizzed by.

'I think I left my stomach behind,' said Ella.

The captain took the wheel and turned the controls so that the ship hung steady. The storm was left far behind, and it was suddenly very quiet.

'Now there's something you don't see twice in a lifetime,' he said.

They clustered round the window. The world had changed. It was blue, and covered with clouds.

The horizon was curved and misty, and behind it the sun was setting. But it was not yellow – it was big and gold, and around it the stars still shone in the deep purple sky.

'Isn't it silent?' said Doggins. 'No wind and rain or thunder?'

'Not up here,' said the captain. 'Nothing ever happens here.'

Just then a shadow slid over the sun, and they heard a chilling noise.

SCREEEECHHHH!

'My blood's gone cold,' said Doggins. 'Just like it says in books!'

The shadow grew nearer and they could all see that it was a gigantic eagle, with huge wings, a dangerous-looking beak and even more dangerous-looking claws. The King Eagle flew down close to the window, and peered in at them. He looked twice as big as the airship.

'If only we had some sort of harpoon—' began Ella.

'No! Leave him alone and he'll go away,' said the captain. 'This is his territory, after all. He's probably wondering what kind of bird we are.'

After dinner the eagle flew away, and the air turned cool as night set in.

'I think we should go down a bit more now,' said the captain, round about tea time. 'It's getting a bit chilly this high up.'

He was interrupted by a long blast from a foghorn and Doggins opened the window.

There, close to them, was another airship sailing through the night sky. It was all black, with a big skull and crossbones in white painted on the gas bag. As they watched, several hatches opened and the snouts of cannons poked out. The foghorn blasted again.

'Stand and deliver!' shouted someone. 'Prepare for boarding! One false move and we'll shoot yer down!'

'Pirates!'

shouted Doggins.

'Stand by to repel boarders,' ordered the captain, seizing a broom. 'If they puncture the gas bag we're done for!'

The black airship drifted nearer, and they could see the pirates peering through the windows. Already they were throwing lines across, and singing triumphant pirate songs:

'Fifteen men on a dead man's chest –
Yo ho ho and a packet of crisps.'

'Any gold or jools?' asked the pirate captain, climbing in through the window.

And suddenly the pirates were everywhere, fighting like mad. The captain waved his broom about and battled the pirates and Ella seized a poker and stood ready to defend the controls of the airship. Doggins found himself out on the veranda, in mortal combat with the pirate chief. Back and forth they fought (Doggins was using a mop). Then the chief cut the mop handle in two and gave Doggins a good push.

Down . . .
down . . .
down . . .

The air went rushing by, and in the darkness he could just make out the two airships getting smaller and smaller above him, while the pirate chief's laughter rang in his ears.

He was turning over and over slowly as he fell down through the clouds, mist all around him.

Wumph! It was like landing on a feather mattress! It *is* a feather mattress, thought Doggins cautiously, feeling around underneath him. What is a mattress doing up here? He crawled out of the feathers and looked around.

The King Eagle turned his head and squinted down at Doggins. 'What are you doing on my back, earth-thing?' he said.

'Please, sire, I was pushed out of our airship,' said Doggins. 'There are pirates up there! I must get back up and help the captain.'

'Pirates, you say? Hold on!' The King Eagle

flapped his wide wings and shot up through the air.

Doggins had thought that the airship had gone up faster than anything he had ever thought was possible, and he had fallen down even faster, but the flight of the King Eagle was like a rocket.

The captain was fighting for his life when he saw a tiny speck rising through the clouds. It grew and grew, and as the King Eagle swept past, the wind blew the airship round and round.

The pirates screamed as they saw the eagle, and raced back along the ropes to their own ship. The captain helped the last one out of the door with a kick, just as the King Eagle seized the pirate ship in his talons and flew off.

Doggins climbed down from the gas bag where the King Eagle had dropped him.

'Well, I'm glad that's over,' he said, dusting himself down. 'Everybody all right?'

They were. But they rapidly let some of the gas out of the airship so that they came back nearer the ground – they didn't quite trust the King Eagle not to snatch them next.

'I think we've had enough excitement for a while,' said the captain. 'Next time we see a peaceful spot, we'll stop and have a rest. Agreed?'

They sailed on until morning, and then the air grew soft and still and the airship came to rest in a clump of brambles. After a little while Ella opened the door and dropped the fishing-line anchor, which caught round the roots of a hawthorn tree.

Doggins stuck his nose out of the window. 'This looks like a nice place,' he said.

They were on a very small island, which was covered in grass and brambles. Quite nearby were hundreds of other islands, all very small, some with houses on. On the roofs of the houses people sat in

long rows, with their possessions gathered around them. They were all very quiet.

'Hey!' shouted the captain to a small boy who was floating by on a log, a bag of newspapers over his shoulder. 'Where is this place?'

'I'm not quite sure. It was a road last time I was here. Excuse me, but I've got to go and deliver my papers.' The boy paddled off between the islands.

'Do you know what I think?' said Ella. 'I think these islands were *hills* until just a little while ago.'

She was right. In the water, all sorts of things were floating – old hen coops, tables, tins, and anything else that could keep people up out of the water. As they watched, a large wicker shopping basket drifted by and got caught in an eddy. Round and round it went, while a small man in a big black hat sat on it and looked miserable.

'Could you dish me out, please?' he cried as he went round yet again.

The captain got a boat hook from the rack over the fireplace, climbed down his rope ladder and carefully lifted the man out of the groceries and helped him up the ladder and into the airship. A little while later the basket sank, and all that remained of it was a floating loaf.

'Oh, it's terrible, terrible,' moaned the little man as they dried him out in front of the fire.

'What on earth's happened?' asked Doggins.

'The big dam up the river has broken. Everyone's flooded out.'

He told them what had happened – how the

flood wave had caught him just when he was leaving the library, and how he had floated all morning with nothing to eat but a tin of baked beans and a cold sausage.

All that day, the airship went from hilltop to hilltop, collecting people who had been flooded out of their homes. Soon the airship was full up, and the captain had to take it down very close to the water. Behind it bobbed a string of boats and receptacles.

'It looks like we've got the entire population with us,' whispered the captain to Doggins. 'Have you any idea what we should do with them?'

Doggins stared out of the window. 'Now there's a place that looks familiar,' he said, pointing to a larger island than the rest of them. It looked very much like his home mountain, and as he got closer he could see his house on it. 'You'd better steer for that,' he sighed, 'though what I shall feed them with I really don't know.'

They anchored, and Doggins led the way into his house. He had been away for several weeks, so it was a bit dusty, and there wasn't very much in the larder. In fact, there was only a sack of beans and a tin of porridge.

'It'll have to be porridged beans, or bean porridge,' he said. 'I don't suppose anyone doesn't fancy any?' he added hopefully.

But after sitting in the cold and wet all day everyone felt that they could face a nice big plateful. So Doggins and the small man in the big

black hat put a big cauldron on the stove, and tried
to find some dry firewood.

Meanwhile, the captain and Ella chugged over
the forest looking for the burst dam.

'There it is!' shouted Ella. 'You can
see the water pouring through the
hole!'

They landed and went to look at the damage. A large boulder had rolled down from the mountain and smashed into it, leaving a large gap. The lake behind the dam was almost empty.

'Poor old Doggins,' said Ella, wringing out her coat. 'Fancy having to look after all those people!'

'Oh, I don't know,' replied the captain. 'I think Doggins is the sort of person who likes to do that sort of thing. He's the sort of person people rely on.'

'Oh, well,' said Ella, and didn't say any more.

They cut down a few trees, then threw ropes down from the airship and pulled the logs over to the hole in the dam. Then Ella gathered lots of twigs and branches from around the lake behind the dam, and they piled them up behind the logs so that they filled up any holes between the logs.

'I think that's that,' said the captain, when they got back to Doggins' house. 'You'll all have to block it up properly one of these days, but it'll do for now.'

Already the water was going down.

'Anyway, we'll be off now, I think,' said the captain. 'Coming, Doggins?'

Doggins looked around at all the washing up. 'I don't think so,' he said slowly. 'There's all this tidying up to do, and we've got to rebuild the dam like you said, and then I'd better make sure everyone's got somewhere to live . . .'

'I see,' said the captain. 'Well, goodbye then, Doggins.' Then they all shook hands, and went back into the airship. Slowly it lifted off, and then drifted away south.

'Well, that *was* a Big Adventure indeed,' Doggins said to himself as he watched the airship until it was lost from sight. 'There and Back, and

Home Again.' Then he rolled up his sleeves and looked around happily.

'**What a lot there is to do,**' he said.

RINCEMANGLE, THE GNOME OF EVEN MOOR

Once upon a time there was a gnome who lived in a hollow tree on Even Moor, the strange mysterious land to the north of Blackbury. His name was Rincemangle and as far as he knew he was the only gnome left in the world.

Real gnomes are very small – only a few centimetres tall – but like all real gnomes Rincemangle didn't look the way many people think a gnome should.*

He wore a pointed hat, of course, because gnomes always do; but apart from that he wore a shabby mouseskin suit and a rather smelly overcoat made from old moleskins. He didn't have a big jolly face, and he certainly didn't have a beard. He lived on nuts and berries and the remains of picnics, and birds' eggs when he could get them. It wasn't a very joyful life.

One day he was sitting in his hollow tree gnawing a hazelnut. It was pouring with rain, and the tree leaked. Rincemangle thought he was getting nasty twinges in his joints.

'Blow this for a lark,' he said. 'I'm wet through and fed up. And a bit lonely. Maybe there are other gnomes in the world . . . ?'

An owl who lived in the tree next door heard him and flew over. 'You should go out and see the

* If you look carefully in the gardens of houses around where you live, you might see an example of what people think gnomes should look like. They often seem to be carrying fishing rods. Which wouldn't be much use in a tree.

world,' he said. 'There's more places than Even Moor. Maybe even more gnomes.' And he told him stories about the streets of Blackbury and places even further away, where the sun always shone and the seas were blue. Actually, they weren't very accurate stories, because the owl had heard about these places from a blackbird who had heard about them from a swallow who went there for his holidays, but they were enough to get Rincemangle feeling very restive.

In less time than it takes to tell, he had packed his few possessions in a handkerchief.

'I'm off!' he cried. 'To places where the sun always shines! How far did you say they were?'

'Er,' said the owl, who hadn't the faintest idea. 'About a couple of miles, I expect. Perhaps a bit more.'

'Cheerio then,' said Rincemangle.

'If you could read I'd send you a postcard.'

He scrambled d$_{own}$ the tree and set off.

When Rincemangle set off down the road to Blackbury he really didn't know how far it was, but it was raining, so he soon got fed up.

After a while he came to a layby. There was a lorry parked there while the driver sat in the cab and ate his packed lunch. Rincemangle had often watched lorries go past on the road near his tree, so he climbed up a tyre and looked for somewhere warm to sleep under the tarpaulin at the back.

The lorry was full of cardboard boxes. He nibbled one open, but found it was just full of horrible tins. They weren't even comfortable to sleep on, but he did eventually drop off, just as the lorry set off again to Blackbury.

When Rincemangle woke up it was very dark

in the box, and there was a lot of banging about going on; then that stopped, and after waiting until all the sounds had died away he peered cautiously through the hole in his box.

The first thing he saw was another gnome, standing below and looking up at him with a friendly smile.

'Hullo,' said the gnome. 'Is there much interesting up there? It looks like another load of baked beans to me. Here, help me get a tin out.' He climbed up to the box rather like a mountaineer – the box was on the top of a pile – and he began to chew.

Together they gnawed at the box until one tin rolled out. They lowered the tin down on a piece of thread.

'My name's Featherhead,' said the gnome. 'You're new here, aren't you? Just up from the country?'

'I thought I was the only gnome in the world,' said Rincemangle.

'Oh, there's a lot of us here. Who wants to live in a hollow tree when you can live in a department store like this?'

Talking and rolling the tin along in front of them they crept out of the storeroom and set off. The store was closed for the night, of course, but a few lights had been left on. There was a rather nasty moment when they had to hide from the lady who cleaned the floors, but after a long haul up some stairs Rincemangle arrived at the gnomes' home.

The gnomes had built themselves a home under the floorboards between the toy shop and the Do-it-yourself department, though they had – er – *borrowed* quite a lot of railway track from the toy shop and built a sort of underground railway all the way to the restaurant area. They even had a phone rigged up between the colony and the gnomes who lived in the Gents' Suiting department two floors down.

All this came as a **great** shock to Rincemangle, of course. When he arrived with his new friend Featherhead, pushing the baked bean tin in front of them, he felt quite out of place. The gnomes lived in small cardboard houses under the floorboards, with holes drilled through the ceiling to let the light in. Featherhead rolled the tin into his house and shut the door.

'Well, this is a cut above my old hollow tree,' said Rincemangle, looking around.

'Everyone's in the restaurant, I expect,' said Featherhead. 'There's about three hundred gnomes living here, you know. My word, I think it's very odd, you living out in all weathers! Most gnomes have lived indoors for years!'

He led Rincemangle along the floor, through a hole in a brick wall and along a very narrow ledge. This was the lift, he explained. Of course, the gnomes could use the big lift, but they'd rigged up a smaller one at the side of the shaft just for themselves. It was driven by clockwork.

They arrived in the Gents' Suiting department after a long ride down the dark shaft. It was brightly lit, and several gnomes were working on a giant sewing machine.

'Good evening!' said one, bustling up, rubbing his hands. 'Hello, Featherhead – what can I do for you?'

'My friend here in the mouseskin trousers . . .' began Featherhead. 'Can't you make him something natty in tweed? We can't have a gnome who looks like he's just stepped out of a mushroom!'

The gnomish tailors worked hard – and speedily. In no time at all, they had made Rincemangle a suit out of a square of cloth in a pattern book and there was enough over for a spare waistcoat.

Featherhead led him back down under the floorboards and they went on to the toy department, where most of the gnomes spent the night (they slept when the store was open during the day).

All the lights were on. Two gnomes were racing model cars around the display stands, while two teams of young gnomes had unrolled one of those big football games and had started playing, while a watching crowd squeaked with excitement.

'Don't any human beings ever come down here at night?' asked Rincemangle, who was a bit shocked. 'I mean, you don't keep lookouts or anything!'

'Oh, no one comes here after the cleaners have gone home,' said Featherhead. 'We have the place to ourselves.'

But they didn't.

You see, the store people had noticed how food disappeared and how things had been moved around in the night. They were sensible people so they didn't believe in gnomes. They thought it was rats, or mice.

So they had bought a cat.

Rincemangle saw it first. He looked up from the football game and saw a big green eye watching them through a partly open door. He didn't know it was a cat, but it looked like a fox – and he knew what foxes were like.

'Run for your lives!'

he bellowed.

Everyone saw the cat as it pushed open the door. With shrill cries of alarm several gnomes rolled back the carpet and opened the trap door to their underground homes, but they were too late.

The cat trotted in and stared at them.

'Stand still now,' hissed Rincemangle. **'He'll get you if you move!'**

Fortunately, perhaps because of the way he said it, the gnomes stood still. Rincemangle thought quickly, and then ran to one of the toy cars the gnomes had been using. As the cat bounded after him he drove away in it.

He wasn't very good at steering, but he managed to drive right out of the toy department – leading the cat away from the other gnomes – before crashing the car into a display of garden tubs. He jumped out and climbed the stem of a potted plant just as the cat dashed up and sprang at the car.

From the topmost leaf Rincemangle was able to jump onto a shelf, and he ran and hid behind a stack of picnic plates – knocking quite a few down in the process, I'm sorry to say.

After half an hour or so, the cat got fed up and wandered off, so Rincemangle was able to climb down.

When he got back to the gnomes' home under the floorboards the place was in uproar. Some families were gathering their possessions together, and several noisy meetings were going on.

Rincemangle found Featherhead packing his belongings into an old tea caddy.

'Oh, hello,' he said. 'I say, that was pretty clever of you, leading the cat away like that!'

'What are you doing?'

'Well, we can't stay here now they've got a cat, can we?' said Featherhead.

But it was even worse than that, because very soon the night watchman who usually stayed downstairs came up and saw all the broken things on the floor, and he called the police.

*

All the next day the gnomes tried to sleep, and when the store emptied for the night the head gnomes called them all together. They decided that the only thing to do was to leave the store. But where could they go?

Rincemangle stood up and said, 'Why don't you go back and live in the country? That's where gnomes used to live.'

They were all shocked. One fat gnome said, 'But the food here is so marvellous. And I've heard that there are wild animals in the country that are even worse than cats!'

'Besides,' someone else said, 'how would we get there? All three hundred of us? It's miles and miles away!'

Just then two gnomes burst in dragging a saucer full of blue powder. It smelled odd, they said. They'd found it in the restaurant.

Rincemangle sniffed at it. 'It's poison,' he said. 'They think we're rats or mice! I tell you, if you don't leave soon you'll all be killed.'

Featherhead said, 'I think he's right. But how can we leave? Think of the roads we'd have to cross, for one thing!'

As the days passed things got worse and worse for the gnomes. Apart from the cat, there were night watchmen patrolling the store after everyone had gone home, and the gnomes hardly dared to show themselves. They certainly couldn't drive around in the toy cars again, or play football.

But they couldn't think of a way to leave. None of them fancied walking through the city with all its dangers. There were the lorries that delivered goods every day, but only a few brave gnomes were prepared to be a stowaway on them – and, besides,

no one knew where they would stop.

'We will have to take so much with us!' moaned the head gnome, sitting sadly on an empty cotton reel. 'String and cloth, and all sorts of things. Food too. A lot of the older gnomes wouldn't survive for five minutes in the country otherwise. We've had such an easy life here, you see.'

Rincemangle scratched his head. 'I suppose so, but you'll have to give it up sooner or later. Where's Featherhead?'

Featherhead had led a raid on the book section to see if there were any books about living in the country that they could take with them. Towards dawn his party of tired gnomes came back, dragging a big paper bag.

'We were almost spotted by the night watchman,' muttered Featherhead. 'We got a few books, though.'

There was one he had put in the sack that had

nothing to do with the country, but it did have a lot of pictures in it, so Rincemangle looked at it.* 'Teach Yourself to Drive,' he read aloud v e r y s l o w l y, working out the words partly by looking at the picture of the human on the front cover, sitting in the front of a car. **'Hmmm.'** He opened it with some difficulty and saw a large picture showing the controls of a car. He didn't say anything for a long time.

Finally the head gnome said: 'It's very interesting, but I hardly think you're big enough to drive anything!'

'No,' said Rincemangle. 'But perhaps . . . Featherhead, can you show me where the lorries are parked at night? I've got an idea . . .'

Early the next evening the two gnomes went to the large underground car park. The journey took them

* He had taught himself to read by looking at bits of paper that had blown over by his tree, most of which had pictures on them too. It meant he knew a lot of useful words like TEAR HERE and FULLY ORGANIC and EXTRA-TASTY WITH ADDED COLOURINGS but he wasn't very good at simple things like 'The dog sat on the mat.'

quite a long time because they had to take turns at dragging the book on driving behind them.

And it took them all night to examine the lorry. When they arrived back at the toy department they were very tired and covered in oil.

Rincemangle called the gnomes together. 'I think we can leave here and take things with us,' he said, 'but it will be rather tricky. We'll have to drive a lorry, you see.'

He drew diagrams to explain. A hundred gnomes would turn the steering wheel by pulling on ropes, while fifty would be in charge of the gear lever. Other groups would push the pedals when necessary, and one gnome would hang from the driving mirror and give commands through a megaphone.

'It looks quite straightforward,' said Rincemangle. 'To me it looks as though driving just involves pushing and pulling things at the right time.'

An elderly gnome got up and said nervously, 'I'm not sure about all this. I'm sure there must be more to driving than that.'

But a lot of the younger gnomes were very enthusiastic,* and so the idea took hold.

For the rest of the week the gnomes were very busy. Some stole bits of string from the hardware department, and several times the most scientific gnomes visited the lorries at night to take measurements and try and find out how they worked. Meanwhile, the older gnomes rolled their possessions down through the store until they were piled up in the ceiling of the lorry garage.

A handpicked party of intrepid mountaineering gnomes found out where the lorry keys were kept (high up on a hook in a little office).

* Especially those who had been driving the model cars in the toy department. After all, how much harder could a big lorry be? Some of those model cars fought back on corners!

Rincemangle, meanwhile, studied road maps and wondered what the *Highway Code* was for.*

At last the day came for moving.

'We've got to work fast,' said Rincemangle, when they heard the last store assistant leave the building at the end of the day. **'Come on – now!'**

While the gnomes lowered their possessions through the garage roof onto the back of the lorry, Rincemangle and an advance party of young gnomes squeezed into the cab through a hole by the brake pedal.

Inside, it was – to them – like being in a big empty hall. The steering wheel seemed very big and far too high up. The gnomes formed themselves into a pyramid, and by standing on the topmost gnome's back Rincemangle managed to throw a line over the steering wheel. Soon they had several rope ladders rigged up and could set to work.

* There were odd signs saying things like ROADWORKS AHEAD. Well, why wouldn't a road work?

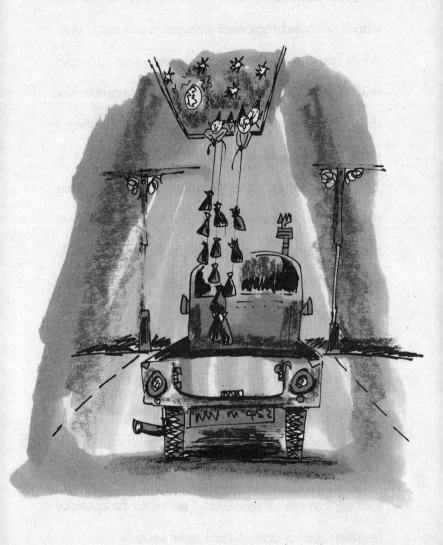

They planned to steer by two ropes tied to the wheel, with fifty gnomes hanging onto each one. While this was being sorted out, other gnomes built a sort of wooden platform up against the windscreen, just big enough for Rincemangle to stand and give orders through a megaphone.

Other gnomes came in and were sent to their positions by Featherhead. Before long the cab was festooned with rope ladders, pulleys and fragile wooden platforms, and these in turn were covered with gnomes hanging onto levers and lengths of thread.

The big moment came when the ignition key was hauled up and shoved into its keyhole by two muscular gnomes. They gave a twist and some lights came on.

'Right,' said Rincemangle, looking down at the waiting crowds. 'Well, this is going to be a tricky business, so let's get started right away.'

Featherhead joined him on the platform and hauled up the *Teach Yourself to Drive* book and a street map of Blackbury.

'On the word Go, the Starter Button party will give it a good press and – er – the Accelerator Pedal squad will press the pedal briefly,' he said uncertainly. 'The gnomes working the clutch and gear lever will stand by. Go!'

Of course, it didn't work as simply as that. It took quite some time before the gnomes found out how to start up properly. But at last the engine was going, making the cab boom like a gong.

'Headlights on! Clutch down! First gear!' Rincemangle shouted above the din. There were several ghastly crashes and the great lorry rolled forward.

'Here, what about the garage doors?' shouted Featherhead.

The lorry rolled onwards. There was a loud **bang** and the doors didn't seem to matter any more. The lorry was out on the street.

'Turn left!' shouted Rincemangle hoarsely. **'Now straighten up!'**

For several minutes the cab was full of shouts and bangs as the gnomes pushed and pulled on the controls. The lorry wove from side to side and went up on the pavement several times, but at least it kept going. Rincemangle even felt bold

enough to order a gear change.

Through the dark streets of Blackbury the lorry swayed and rumbled, occasionally bouncing off lampposts. Every now and again there was a horrible **clonk** as it changed gear.

Steering was the big difficulty. By the time the gnomes down below had heard Rincemangle's order it was usually too late. It was a good job there were no other vehicles on the road at that time of night, or there would have been a very nasty accident.

They blundered through the traffic lights and into Blackbury High Street, knocking a piece off a letter box. Featherhead was staring into the great big mirror, high above them, that showed what traffic was behind.

'There's a car behind with a big blue flashing light on it,' he said conversationally. 'Listen! It's making a siren noise.'

'Very decorative, I'm sure,' said Rincemangle, who wasn't really listening. 'Look lively down below! It's a straight road out of town now, so change into top gear.'

There was a **thud** and a *crash*, but the gnomes were getting experienced now and the lorry whizzed away, still weaving from side to side.

'The car with the flashing lights keeps trying to overtake us,' said Featherhead. 'Gosh! We nearly hit it that time!' He craned up and had another look. 'There's two human beings in peaked caps inside it,' he added. 'Golly! They look furious!'

'I expect someone has got a little angry because of all those lampposts we knocked down. I don't think we were supposed to,' said Rincemangle. Unfortunately, while he said this, he didn't look where they were going . . .

The lorry rumbled off the road and straight through a hedge. The field behind it was ploughed, and the gnomes had to hang on tightly as they were jolted around in the cab.

The police car screeched to a halt and the two policemen started running across the field after them, shouting.

The lorry went through another hedge and frightened a herd of cows.

Rincemangle peered through the window. There

was a wood ahead, and behind that the heather-clad slopes of Even Moor started climbing up towards the sky.

'Prepare to abandon lorry!'

he shouted. They plunged into a wood and the lorry stopped dead in the middle of a bramble thicket. It was suddenly very quiet.

Then there was a very busy five minutes as the gnomes unloaded their possessions from the back of the lorry. By the time the policemen arrived there was not a gnome to be seen. Rincemangle and Featherhead were sitting high up on a bramble branch and watched as the men wandered around the abandoned lorry, scratching their heads. After poking around inside the cab and finding the little ropes and ladders they wandered away, arguing.

When they had gone the gnomes crept out of their hiding places and gathered around Rincemangle.

'Even Moor is only a short walk away,' he said. 'Let's spend the day hidden here and we can be up there by tonight!'

The gnomes lit fires and settled down to cook breakfast. They made cups of tea and handed them round and they all toasted their new home. Many of them were wondering what it would be like to live in the country again after so long in the town. A lot of the little ones, of course – I mean, even littler than the average gnome – were rather looking forward to it. But they all knew that there was going to be a lot of hard work before them.

Early next morning a poacher, coming home for breakfast, told his wife he'd seen a lot of little lights climbing up the slopes of the Moor.

She didn't believe him.

Perhaps you will.

For more stories from the fantastically funny
TERRY PRATCHETT you might like to try

DRAGONS
at Crumbling Castle
and other stories

**Keep reading for a look at
one of the stories . . .**

DRAGONS AT CRUMBLING CASTLE

In the days of King Arthur there were no newspapers, only town criers, who went around shouting the news at the tops of their voices.

King Arthur was sitting up in bed one Sunday, eating an egg, when the Sunday town crier trooped in. Actually, there were several of them: a man to draw the pictures, a jester for the jokes and a small man in tights and football boots who was called the Sports Page.

'DRAGONS INVADE CRUMBLING CASTLE,'

shouted the News Crier (this was the headline), and then he said in a softer voice, **'For full details hear page nine.'**

King Arthur dropped his spoon in amazement. **Dragons!** All the knights were out on quests, except for Sir Lancelot – and he had gone to France for his holidays.

The Ninth Page came panting up, coughed, and said: 'Thousands flee for their lives as family of green dragons burn and rampage around Crumbling Castle . . .'

'What is King Arthur doing about this?' demanded the Editorial Crier pompously. 'What do we pay our taxes for? The people of Camelot demand action . . .'

'Throw them out, and give them fourpence* each,' said the king to the butler. 'Then call out the guard.'

Later that day he went out to the courtyard.

'Now then, men,' he said. 'I want a volunteer . . .' Then he adjusted his spectacles. The only other person in the courtyard was a small boy in a suit of mail much too big for him.

'Ralph reporting, sire!' the lad said, and saluted.

'Where's everyone else?'

'Tom, John, Ron, Fred, Bill and Jack are off

---

* In the days of King Arthur, this was a lot more money than it seems today – it would buy, oh, at least a cup of mead and a hunk of goat's meat.

sick,' said Ralph, counting on his fingers. 'Then William, Bert, Joe and Albert are on holiday. James is visiting his granny. Rupert has gone hunting. And Eric . . .'

'Well then,' said the king. 'Ralph, how would you like to visit Crumbling Castle? Nice scenery, excellent food, only a few dragons to kill. Take my spare suit of armour – it's a bit roomy, but quite thick . . .'

So Ralph got on his donkey and trotted over the drawbridge, whistling, and disappeared over the hills. When he was out of sight he took off the armour and hid it behind a hedge, because it squeaked and was too hot, and put on his ordinary clothes.

High on a wooded hill sat a mounted figure in coal-black armour. He watched the young boy pass by, then galloped down after him on his big black horse.

'HALT IN THE NAME OF THE FRIDAY KNIGHT,'

he cried in a deep voice, raising his black sword.

Ralph looked round. 'Excuse me, sir,' he said. 'Is this the right road to Crumbling Castle?'

'Well, yes, actually it is,' said the knight, looking rather embarrassed, and then he remembered that he was really a big bad knight, and continued in a hollow voice,

'BUT YOU'LL HAVE TO FIGHT ME FIRST!'

Ralph looked up in amazement as the black knight got off his horse and charged at him, waving his sword.